Invisible String

Fanny Temple

Contents

Prologue 1

Chapter 1 3

Chapter 2 8

Chapter 3 15

Chapter 4 24

Chapter 5 32

Chapter 6 42

Chapter 7 53

Chapter 8 60

Chapter 9 67

Chapter 10 74

Chapter 11 80

Chapter 12 90

Chapter 13 97

Chapter 14 105

Chapter 15											111

Chapter 16											119

Chapter 17											127

Chapter 18											132

Chapter 19											139

Chapter 20											146

Chapter 21											151

Chapter 22											159

Chapter 23											165

Chapter 24											173

Chapter 25											179

Prologue

C offee filled the cups of the officers sitting around the table in the conference room. Files were given, notes being taken and things underlined. His golden eyes glanced around the room, excitement filling him as he awaited the next assignment.

Rumor has it a well known family is moving to Republic City. The couple being close personal friends with the president himself. The high profile of the family naturally made them a target, so Chief Beifong was itching to get them safely settled into their penthouse apartment on the Upper East side of the city.

The meeting dragged on, Mako catching himself zoning out a couple of times out the window. It was just a briefing on the families arrival to port, the president greeting them at the docks for a few photos before the family would be ushered into cabbies and taken to their new home.

Things had been calm in Republic City. After Unalaq and Vaatu were taken care of, things seemed to have leveled out. Korra was off visiting the Air Temples with Tenzin and his family, doing whatever avatars do. Which let team avatar slide back into their normal routines. Asami went to work on her father's company.... Or her company now. Mako's younger brother,

Bolin, was doing spirit knows what. He was busy bouncing around from studio to studio working on movers.

And now, Mako sat in a meeting going over formalities for the president's entry and exit to meet this famous family.

What had his life become?

Chapter 1

My heart was pounding, small beads of sweat forming on my forehead as I glanced over to my sisters. The door to the ship was about to be opened, the sounds of people chatting and photos being taken echoing around the chamber.

"How is my hair?" my sister whispered, leaning to glance at her reflection in the metal door.

"You look fine, Vera" my father smiled, patting her shoulder. "Don't stress."

"How can I not stress, daddy?" Vera whined. "The entire city is about to see me after two weeks at sea!"

"Looks more like two months!" My little sister Bo giggled, blue eyes gleaming in mischief.

Vera rolled her eyes, my father chuckling softly to himself as we got ready to leave the ship. I inhale, fingers gripping the fabric of my dress as I watch as the door is opened and the sounds of people cheering ring in my ears.

Flashes spark around me as my father leads us out, the president happily greeting him at the end of the walkway. They shake hands, people cheering as photographers yell our names, begging for a photo.

Vera grins, waving poshly at the cameras as I grab Bo's hand, more for my own security than hers.

"Dr. Shen!" president Raiko grinned, bringing my father into his arms.

The two men talked, shaking hands as people around us took photos. My sisters stood behind, keeping still as we watched the interaction.

"Lei, I could not be happier to have you in my beautiful city" The president grinned, "You'll find Republic City is a place of prosperity and charm."

My father smiled, "I'm happy to call it my new home"

Raiko turned to us, greeting my sisters and I kindly before ushering us to the car that was waiting to take us to our new home.

"Lei, I'd like you to meet Chief Lin Beifong" the president announced, presenting a stern looking woman in a police uniform. "I trust Lin with my life, and I am confident she will keep you and your family safe."

My father shook her hand, greeting the woman as he gestures to us.

"Chief Beifong, these are my three daughters: Vera, Elena, and Bo."

She goes down the line and greets us, nodding her head formally as she turns to her group of officers.

"These are my top officers: Kiel, Meilin, and Mako." She presents, "They will do anything within their power to ensure you and your daughters feel safe and unbothered here in Republic City."

I feel Vera nudge my side, her head leaning close as she whispers in my ear.

"The young one is kinda cute" she giggles.

My eyes scan the line of officers, the third one was around my age. His hair was short and well kept, his golden eyes watching the Chief talk as he stood professionally alongside his colleagues. A small blush creeps on my cheeks, fingers fidgeting as I look away. The faint sound of Vera's giggles taunting me.

After a few minutes of handshakes and photos, my father ushers us into the car.

Bo climbs in first, Vera following behind as I step up and try to climb in. But my dress gets caught under my shoe and I slip, almost knocking my head against the side of the car if a hand doesn't reach up and catch my shoulder.

I gasp, adrenaline pumping as I look to my left, the honey colored eyes of the young officer staring back at me.

"Are you alright?" he asks, voice deep and husky.

I swallow, nodding quickly as I reach down and fix my dress.

"Thank you" I whisper, nodding to the officer as I slide into the seat and sigh, Bo already in fits of laughter.

"Jeez Elena!" She howls, "You're red as a tomato!"

I slump back in the seat, hands over my face as the car roars to life.

Soon the ports turned to the city streets, people moving about their days as we drove to our new home. I had never been to Republic City before, my mind wondering as I took in the scenery outside.

My family and I had bounced from town to town my entire life. My parent's work calling them across the globe. I had never lived in the same place for more than a few years, but somehow we had never made it to Republic City.

Now, my parents were establishing their own clinic, an attempt to settle down and in hopes to try and give us a taste of a normal life. Although Vera and I were grown, perhaps Bo would benefit from being around the same school for more than a year or two.

After minutes of driving we stop in front of a grand building, tall glass windows lining the bottom floor as a doorman smiled and opened the car doors. Vera is first out, eyes wide in excitement as she turns and takes in the city around her.

"This is so much better than the Southern Water Tribe" She states, grabbing her bag and slinging it over her shoulder as she makes her way inside.

I slide out after Bo, my father already speaking to the driver as workers came to grab our bags from the boot of the car.

"This place stinks" Bo whined, making a face.

I stifle a laugh, patting her head, "That is just how the city smells"

Bo frowns, running to catch up with my father as we make our way inside the lobby.

The lobby was grand, lights hanging from the ceiling as various people sat around on the couches. Two men worked the elevators, greeting us with a bow before we stepped in.

My father presses level 20 and we ride all the way up.

The elevator stops and we arrive at a large wooden set of double doors. My father steps forward and unlocks the door, pushing the doors open with a grin.

"Welcome home, girls"

My mouth drops, my feet stepping in and my eyes scanning the marvelous view. The doors opened to a parlor, the walls a smooth white and gold. On the back wall was a large row of floor to ceiling windows, the view of the city breathtaking. In front of the windows sat my piano, the movers positioning my seat so I could turn to my right and look out the large windows.

"This is the life" Vera sighs, flopping on the large gold colored couch.

"Wow!" Bo calls from another room, "My bed is HUGE!"

"Dad, this is incredible" I smile, my father proudly standing beside me.

"I'm glad you like it" He nods, "I made sure to have the piano tuned before you arrived"

I smile, leaning to press my fingers on a few keys, the sound perfect.

"Thank you Dad, for everything" I say, "Mom is going to love it when she gets here"

"I hope so" he chuckled, patting my back. "I hope so"

Chapter 2

The fire was crackling in the fireplace as we sat and drank tea in the parlor. The game board was sat on the table as cards and pieces were lazily tossed around. Vera sat on the couch, cards in her thin fingers as she looked at her hand.

"Go to square 3" Bo announced, reaching over to grab a card.

Vera huffed, reaching over to move her piece before rolling the dice.

"12" I say, "Bo, you're call"

"Vera, go to 7" Bo grinned, knowing exactly what she was doing.

Vera groaned, grabbing her piece and placing it on the square.

"You are an evil, evil little girl" Vera stated, glaring at her.

I open my mouth to say something as a knock on the door sounds.

"I'll get it" I state, "Try not to kill each other"

I place my cards on the floor and hold my dress in my hand as I stand up, moving to the door and opening. I am greeted with a bow, Chief Beifong and an officer standing on the other side.

"Miss Shen" she greets, "Is your father here?"

"No ma'am" I shake my head. "He's down setting things up at his clinic"

"That's not a problem" She nods, "I am just here to deliver his licence plates. We went ahead and got his car registered."

She hands me a thick envelope, stepping aside to reveal the same officer from the other day behind her. I feel my cheeks flush as I look down, the envelope in my hands.

"T-thank you" I stutter, "I'll make sure to give it to him"

"Wonderful" Lin nods, her manner serious. "Well, we'll be going"

She turns to leave, the officer flashing me a smile as he turns and follows her down the hallway and back to the elevator. I shut the door, turning to lean my back against it.

"You are so not smooth" Vera snorts, walking up to me. "You should have said something to him"

"No way" I shake my head quickly, "I don't know how to talk to men"

"It's not any different than talking to regular people" Vera says, crossing her arms. "You just have to smile and twirl your hair, and then he's all yours"

I nervously bite the inside of my cheek, thinking. Vera had a point. I've seen her around men before. She was some sort of siren. Every man she meets she had under her charm in minutes.

Of course, Vera was beautiful. A young heiress with a good head on her shoulders surely made any man melt. Her hair was long and brown, her eyes big and blue like our mother. Although she didn't get our mother's bending, she made up for it everywhere else.

Vera had this ora to her that was intoxicating to men. She was charming, sweet, and intelligent. She could hold a conversation on anything, she knew someone in every place we went, and was beautiful enough to attract attention from even the highest of generals.

Her latest fling was with General Iroh II in the United Forces army. Not only was he the youngest general in the army, but his grandfather was Fire Lord Zuko. Needless to say my father was thrilled when she brought him home for dinner.

I snap back to reality, my sister standing in front of me with her hands on her hips.

"El, were you even listening to me?" She frowns.

"Yea, you told me to twirl my hair and he'll fall in love with me or something" I mumble, walking over to slump in a chair.

"I would just start with saying hello and not staring at him" She laughs,

"Saying hi" I think a loud, "I can do that."

A week later I was shoving the door open of the Republic City Conservatory. The night breeze made me shiver as I snuggled closer to the fabric of my coat. I slung my bag over my shoulder, unlocking my bike and wheeling it around to the side walk.

It was night time now, the streets a lot calmer then when I arrived this afternoon. I was rehearsing for a recital the director was putting on. He was over the moon to find out I had moved here and invited me in for an audition a few days after I arrived.

Now, I was the main act of the recital benefiting the schools of Republic City, a charity event a lot of important people attend. I was thrilled to be a part of it, and even more thrilled to find my mother would be back in time to see the show.

I push off from the ground, my feet on the pedals as I ride down the street, weaving in and out of light posts as I ride down the pavement. I watch people walk by, store shops closing for the night as I turn the corner. I was getting the hang of finding my way around the city, thankfully.

The blue blinking light on top of a car caught my attention, making me slow my speed as I ride up to the officer placing a paper on some poor person's car.

"Officer Mako?" I call, leaning my foot on the ground to stop myself.

He looks up, bowing politely as he steps forward.

"Good evening, Miss Shen"

I smile, brushing a strand of hair behind my ear.

"How are you?"

"I'm well" He nods, shoving his notebook into his shirt pocket. "Just writing my nightly tickets"

"Sounds like fun" I giggle, Vera's words of advice coaching me.

Keep smiling!

"It's a blast" He says sarcastically, his voice playful. "What are you doing biking at this hour?"

"I'm on my way home from rehearsal at the conservatory" I say, "I'm playing in the benefit"

His eyes widen, expression surprised.

"Hey, that's great!" He says, "What do you play?"

"Piano" I smile.

The sound of people yelling in an alley catches both of our attention, Mako's smile turning to a frown. I turn my attention back to him, eyebrows raised.

"Do you want a ride home?" He asks, expression suddenly serious.

I blink in surprise, suddenly nervous.

"Sure" I say, swinging my leg off my bike.

He steps up, taking my bike and wheeling it to the flatbed of his police cart as I slide into the passenger seat. I watch in the mirror as he looks around, a look of concern on his face as he walks over to his side and slides in.

I watch him take out the key and the engine roars to life, Mako moving the wheel and the kart slowly moving into the street.

"So" He says, eyes flashing to check his mirror, "How long have you been playing piano?"

"Forever" I chuckle, "I started when I was a little girl, my parents were gifted a piano by the Fire Lord and I fell in love instantly"

We pass buildings and people walking, slowly stopping at red lights and moving forward when it turns green. The rumble of the engine serving as background music on our drive.

"Do you play any instruments?" I ask, turning to gaze at him.

"No" He shakes his head, eyes focused on the road before us. "I was too busy getting into trouble to play any instruments"

I let out a soft laugh, an amused look on his face.

"I didn't label you as the type to get into trouble"

He glances over at me, his hand moving to shift the car into another gear.

"You'd be surprised" He muses, "I wasn't always the police officer type"

I raise an eyebrow, genuinely curious. Mako had always given off an air of obedience. He was always professional and put together, it was hard to see him in a rebellious sense.

"It's hard to picture that" I say honestly, eyes scanning around the world outside.

"Well, my brother and I were orphaned when I was eight." Mako began, his facial expression serious. "Neither of us knew of any family so we lived on the streets our whole life. In order to survive, we sometimes had to do things I'm not proud of."

I frown, my mind reeling at his information.

"I-I had no idea," I whisper. "I'm so sorry that happened to you"

Mako shrugs, glancing over to me.

"Don't be sorry" He says, "I learned a lot from living on the streets, I think it gave me something I wouldn't have gotten otherwise"

I nod, licking my lips nervously as we pull up to my building. Mako slides out, the doorman rushing up and opening the passenger door for me. I step out, Mako wheeling my bike to me.

"Thank you" I smile, adjusting my bag on my shoulder.

"Don't mention it" Mako shrugs, hand scratching the back of his neck. "Have a good night"

"You as well" I nod, watching him bow gently before climbing back into his police kart.

I turn and begin to wheel my bike inside when I hear him call out.

"Hey! Miss Shen!"

I turn, confused as I lean my bike against the stone wall of the building and move to stand outside his kart. He reaches over and turns the lever as the window rolls down, his body leaning over the seat.

"Listen, if you have any other rehearsals that run late, call me and maybe I can pick you up so you don't have to ride your bike this late at night"

My mouth opens in surprise, nodding my head.

I pinch my leg to stop the butterflies from flying around in my stomach. I'm sure my cheeks are flushed, thank goodness it's dark out.

"Sure" I smile, "Thank you!"

"Here" he mumbles, reaching into his pocket and tearing off a slip of paper. I watch him reach over and grab a pen, his teeth clasping the cap as he pulls the pen out and scribbles on the paper. I watch his face as he writes, eyebrows pulled together in thought as he puts the pen back and hands the paper to me.

"Call me at the station when you get your rehearsal schedule, we can set something up"

I look down at the paper then back to him, "I will, thank you"

"I'll see you around"

I step back as he turns the key and turns to go back onto the street, his kart joining the traffic as I stand dumbly in front of the building with a giant smile on my face.

Chapter 3

I bite my finger nails nervously, leg bouncing up and down as I stare at the telephone in front of me. It had been a day since Mako drove me home, and I've been too nervous to dial his number.

I had rehearsal at the conservatory tonight, so this was the perfect opportunity to call, but the nervousness in my body made my hands sweat and I couldn't muster the courage to make the phone call.

I stare at the slip of paper in my hand, his name and phone number quickly written out on the paper before me. His handwriting was neat, each letter well written and legible. It was yet another part of him I was starting to become fascinated by.

Eversince the conversation in his police kart I haven't been able to stop thinking about it.

Mako? A rebel?

I couldn't believe it. Sure, it was none of my business but I was dying to learn more about him and his past. Everything about this mysterious police officer seemed to strike me with curiosity.

With a strong inhale I grab the phone, fingers dialing each number as I hold it up to my ear and wait. Within a few seconds someone picks up, my stomach bursting into butterflies.

"Republic City Police, this is Officer Mako"

"Mako" I smile, his voice sounding like velvet. "It's Elena Shen"

"Miss Shen" He replies, his voice seeming to perk up. Or maybe I was just imagining things.... "How are you?"

"I'm doing well" I smile, fingers playing with the cord of the phone. "I have rehearsal tonight at the conservatory. It should let out around 9:30"

"That sounds great, I can meet you out front," Mako declares.

"You can come early if you'd like" I muse, confused where this sudden burst of confidence came from. "I can show you around backstage, if you'd like"

"That sounds like fun" Mako says kindly, "How early should I be there?"

"9 o'clock?"

"Perfect" He replies, "I'll see you then"

"See you"

I hang up the phone, a small squeal of happiness coming from my lips as I jump up.

I had so much to do!

Hours later I sit at my vanity, dabbing the cotton sponge on my cheek delicately as I study myself in the mirror. I was never one to put on makeup, so I had to make sure this looked good.

A small knock comes from my door, the sound of chuckles making me turn.

"Since when do you put on rouge for rehearsal?" Vera smirked, leaning against the doorframe.

I blush, looking down.

I've been caught.

"Oh.. um" I brush my hair back, my sister's eyes widening.

"Is that a fresh coat of nail polish?" She quizzes, "El, what is going on?"

"It's nothing" I claim, nervously placing the sponge back in the compact.

"Oh please" Vera taunts, "I know when you're lying. Tell me"

I watch her stroll over to my bed, plopping down on the mattress as she looks at me in the mirror.

"Officer Mako is coming to the conservatory after rehearsal," I announced.

Her blue eyes widen again, mouth dropping in surprise.

"Is that the cute cop that follows the chief around?"

"Mhm" I hum, "Don't make a big deal out of it"

"How can I not?" Vera claims, "Why is he coming to your piano rehearsal?"

"Because he offered to drive me home afterwards so I don't have to ride my bike alone at night"

Vera's lips turn into a smirk, eyes squinting at me.

"He likes you"

"What? No way" I wave her off, "He barely knows me"

"Doesn't matter!" Vera shrugs, "He is a cop, his job is to protect you from robbers or something, not be your personal driver. Clearly he is doing this because he likes you"

"Or he is just dedicated to his job" I reason.

There was no way Mako liked me. He was way out of my league anyway. Besides, who am I to assume he didn't have a girlfriend already?

Vera snorts.

"He's a cop, Elena. Those guys barely get paid enough to buy dinner. Do you think he's going above and behind with that pay grade?"

I shrug, looking down at my hands.

"He really likes his job. He's passionate about it"

Vera shrugs, standing from the bed.

"Whatever you say, El" she hums tauntingly. "Let me know when he makes a move"

I blush, watching her leave.

Mako wouldn't make a move on me? Would he?

-Mako's POV-

I had been sitting in this kart for hours. My eyes scanning the seemingly empty street outside the conservatory. Something within me told me to go early and just watch, to make sure no harm came to the building on anyone who was inside.

Including Elena Shen.

Jeez, I'm such a dork.

I have talked to her once. Only one real conversation and she had been sticking to my mind like a curse. She was everywhere. I tried to file paperwork and her green eyes kept creeping into my head like a sick joke. How was I supposed to function like this?

I was only doing my job.

That was all I was here to do. My job.

I glance at my watch, 9:00 slowly rolling around as I slipped out of my car, making my way up the stairs and into the grand entry of the conservatory. It was my first time inside, I remember sleeping on the front steps as a child, but I was never lucky enough to see the interior.

I slip past the door and into the concert hall, the lights dimmed as only a few lights lit up the stage. There, sat at the black piano was a girl. Her long brown hair was tied into a loose bun as she marked notes on the pages in front of her.

Then before I could even catch my breath, she began to play.

I had heard the piano before, but never like this.

The notes started light and high, her fingers quieting pushing on the keys as she swayed her body to the music. I could see her eyes closing, her body moving ever so slightly with each chord she hit.

A small hit of silence and she was back again, her fingers pressing the keys harder as the notes grew louder and more bold. The music seemed to dance around her, the notes so beautiful and intoxicating I could hardly remember that I was standing in the entryway like an idiot.

Her head swayed with the music, hands quickly reaching up to turn pages as she kept her hands moving quickly up and down the keys. She was in her own world, and I was finding myself so enthralled by it I couldn't help but stare.

Suddenly the music stopped, her head turning to me with a smile.

"You're right on time!" she called, waving me up to the stage.

It took me a few moments to remember how to walk, my feet carrying me down the isle and up the stairs. Her smiling face became clearer.

"That was.... Incredible" I exhale, "Did you compose that yourself?"

She looks down, nodding gently.

"I did, yeah" She smiles, "Did you like it?"

"I loved it" I say, maybe too excitedly. Her cheeks seem to turn red as her eyes flicker down.

"How long did that take you to write?" I ask, shoving my hands nervously in my pockets.

She shrugs, "A few weeks or so. I had to edit it and make sure it sounded nice. But I think it'll work for the benefit"

"It's great," I enthuse.

She replies with a thank you, her green eyes brightening in excitement.

"Here" She waves, "I'll teach you a few chords"

I watch her scoot over on the bench, allowing me to sit on it beside her. I feel my shoulder brush against hers, eyes dumbly scanning the sheet music in front of us.

"I have no idea what any of that means" I confess, a small chuckle coming from her.

"It's really messy" She mumbles, "Most people wouldn't be able to under-stand it either"

I laugh, placing my fingers on the keys beside hers. Her thin hands rest over the keys, her fingers pressing down on a few of them at once.

"This is a C major" she announces, the sound of the keys echoing around the room.

"I have no idea how to do that" I laugh, trying to position my fingers like hers.

She laughs, reaching her left hand over mine and moving it over a few keys so they are resting in a new position.

"Press these three" She hums, pressing on my fingers so I'm hitting three new ivory keys.

I took a moment to admire how slim and small her fingers were compared to mine. There were so smooth and neat, unlike my hands that were cluttered with scars from numerous fights.

"Is this it?" I ask, looking down.

"Mhm" She hums, "C major"

"I'm feeling like a professional already" I chuckle.

She smiles, moving my fingers again and sliding them over the keys, this time resting on two ivory keys and a skinny black one.

"This is D major"

The sound echos around the room, my eyes watching her hands cup my own. I focus on my nerves, trying to keep the heat of my hands down.

I glance up at her, her eyes cast down to our hands as I study her face close up. She had a small nose, freckles littering her skin as her eyelashes were long and curled. I inhale and smell the scent of lavender, the smell calming my nervous as I brush my shoulder against hers.

She looks up, green eyes catching mine as she stares back at me. Her lips were pink and plump, a small set of dimples appearing on her cheeks as she blinks.

"Officer Mako" She says softly, seemingly in a trance.

"Just call me Mako" I whisper back, a small smile on my lips.

"Only if you call me Elena" She teases, green eyes flickering down.

I look down at her lips then back to her eyes, head slowly leaning in as my hand on the piano flips and grabs her small one, the sound of a few keys being hit falling silent on my ears as I watch her close her eyes.

I was about to brush my lips to hers when the sound of a door slamming made her jump, her hand breaking from mine as she brushed her hair behind her ear.

I cough, sitting back as we turn to see a stage worker come into view.

"Elena" the woman says kindly, "I just have a few questions about your backdrop for the benefit"

"Sure" Elena says, her cheeks a deep red as she slides off the bench. "I'll be right there"

The worker nods, turning and walking away before Elena turns to me, eyes cast down at her sheet music.

"I can meet you in the car" I suggest.

She nods, giving me a small smile as she clears her throat.

"I'll be out soon" She says quickly, shoving the papers into her bag and hurrying off the side of the stage.

I turn back to the keys, placing my fingers in the spot she taught me before pressing down.

"D major" I whisper to myself.

Chapter 4

It was almost daybreak, the sun beginning to rise over the towers in the city skyline. I sighed, resting my elbow on the side of the piano as I laid my head in my hand. My eyes lost focus on the outdoors, my mind wondering back the night before.

We were inches apart. I could smell his cologne, a rich woody scent laced with the smell of soap. His breath fanned over my face, my heart nearly beat out of my chest.

I was up all night, restless in bed as I laid awake.

I should have said more. I should have mentioned it on the ride home.

After I finished my conversation with the stage mangers I met him in his police kart, not another word was spoken about the almost-sorta-maybe-kiss that happened in the concert hall.

He kept our minds busy with questions about the benefit, and useless information about the guestlist. I didn't care about who was coming, all I could think or care about was him.

He almost kissed me.

If we didn't get interrupted would he have done it?

The way his hand grabbed mine, the sour sounding keys being pushed meant nothing in that moment. It was like something out of a daydream.

Just for a split moment I saw him with his eyes closed, lips pursed as he leaned into me. He was gorgeous, beyond something I could have drawn up in a dream.

I look down at my hands, the light pink polish still smooth under the creeping sunlight. I trace the ivory keys with my fingers, a small laugh coming when I think back to showing him how to play a D major chord.

He was so clueless when it came to the piano, but something about that enchanted me even more. He was so excited to learn about it, so eager to listen.

A faint smile crosses my lips at the memory, the events still so recent I could almost feel the heat radiating off the top of his hand into my palms.

Hours later I'm woken up to someone shaking me. Startled, my eyes widen as Vera stands in her nightgown looking down at me.

"Did you sleep here all night?" she asks, standing straight as I sit up.

I nod, rubbing the back of my neck.

"I don't remember lying down here" I confess, my back suddenly aching from sleeping on the cramped couch.

"How was your rehearsal with Mako?" Vera asks, plopping herself into the arm chair across from me.

I smile, hands dancing around the fabric of my nightgown.

"He almost kissed me"

Vera's blue eyes widen in shock, a look of surprise crossing her face.

"Wow, El" she snickers, "I didn't think you had in ya"

I blush, standing from my spot as I move to go into the kitchen. I needed tea.

"We didn't actually kiss though" I frown, pulling a cup from the drawer. "We were interrupted"

"So he's definitely into you" Vera announces, leaning against the counter.

I shrug, "It could have been a spir of the moment"

Vera rolls her eyes, my hands going to collect the kettle to heat some water.

"Men don't just kiss women randomly if they aren't interested in them" She lectures, "Especially without any wine in their system."

A smile graces my lips as I look down at the kettle.

She was right. He did want to kiss me.

Moments later my father strolls in, already dressed for the day.

"Morning" He greets, kissing both of our foreheads. "I am going to be out for the afternoon, I have a meeting down at the clinic"

"Alright" Vera smiles, "Do you want us to pick up Bo?"

"That would be wonderful, yes" He nods, "Her school ends at 2"

We nod, watching him hurry out of the kitchen with a thermos of coffee.

"Mail is here" He calls from the other room, the sound of the door closing telling us we were now alone.

I pour two cups, placing tea bags in both as I follow my sister into the parlor. I set them down, watching as she shifts through the letters brought by the morning mail run.

She stops on the last one, face changing from bored to serious. She drops the other envelopes on the table and sits down beside me.

"What's wrong?" I hum, sipping the hot drink.

"It's a letter from Iroh" Vera whispers, fingers holding the tan colored envelope.

"Are you going to open it?" I ask, noting her sad expression.

"I don't know" she whispers, sad eyes studying the handwriting.

Iroh and Vera were a couple when we were staying in the Fire Nation a few years back. They met the first week we were there when we were having dinner with Fire Lord Zuko and hit it off right away. My parents were convinced they were going to get married. But his busy schedule with the United Forces took him all around the world, not allowing him much time for love or for Vera.

So he ended things the day before we were set to leave. Vera wasn't over it for a long time. I still wonder if she truly is now.

I pat her shoulder, watching her quickly reach up to wipe her eyes with her sleeve.

"I'll leave you alone" I whisper, standing from the couch and going into the kitchen.

After an hour I come out of my room, dressed for the day as I move back into the parlor. Vera was sitting stone faced in front of the fire, the thin slip of paper between her fingers. I could tell she had been crying, her cheeks puffy and eyelids red.

I sit beside her, hand on her shoulder as she sniffs.

"I'm alright" She declared, clearing her throat.

"What did he say?" I ask gently, watching her stand from the couch.

"Nothing of note" She shrugged, arms folded on her chest. "He wanted to make sure we were settled in and that I was happy"

I nod, biting my cheek. I was never good at giving relationship advice, saying I had never been in a relationship before.

"I don't want to dwell on it" She states, "Let's do something fun"

I nod, standing beside her.

"Like what?"

She walks to the window, eyes peering out over the bustling city.

"We have this whole city at our fingertips, let's do some exploring!"

We walked down the busy streets of Republic City, our arms locked together as we window shopped and discovered the sights of our new home. It was a lot busier than I had expected it to be. I always thought Ba Sing Se was the craziest place in the world, but Republic City had taken the crown.

People were everywhere, cars roaring by on the street as we weaved through crowds of merchants and families. Vera had bought a few new outfits, declaring "Shopping was the best medicine." She picked out silk skirts and ruffled tops, a few pieces of jewelry and a new scarf.

Now, after what felt like our 100th store, we settled at a small cafe to enjoy warm cups of jasmine tea. We sat on the patio under the cloth tent roof, people passing by on the street as we took in the sights and sounds of the city.

"I can't believe you didn't find anything you liked" Vera mused, sitting across from me with her pile of bags.

I shrug, stirring my tea.

"I didn't see anything that called to me" I say, "I am still looking for a gown to wear to the benefit"

"Are you going to invite Mako?" She asks, lips curling into a smirk.

Leave it to your big sister to tease the daylights out of you.

"I don't know" I confess, "I don't want to rush things. It could be awkward"

Vera waves it off, "I'm sure he'd be thrilled to go."

I open my mouth to protest but the sound of yelling makes us turn. On the sidewalk stood Mako. He was dressed in grey, out of his police uniform as he whispers harshly to the man beside him.

My eyes widen, pulse rising as Vera sends me a quick smirk.

"Come join us!" She calls, waving the men over.

I kick her under the table and hear her hiss in pain as the boys make their way over to us.

"Elena" Mako smiles

"Hey, Mako" I reply, "This is my sister, Vera. I'm not sure if you have properly met"

"Nice to finally meet you" Vera grins, shaking his hand as I roll my eyes.

"This is my brother, Bolin" Mako introduces, "Bolin, this is Elena and Vera Shen. Dr. Shen's daughters"

"Pleasure to meet you ladies" Bolin grins.

Bolin was a little shorter than Mako, his smile a little goofier as I could tell he was the less-serious one of the two.

"So, what brings you to our side of town?" Mako asks, turning to me.

"We were shopping" I say, "Vera suggested we do some exploring."

"There is a great store a few blocks that way" Bolin suggested, "Sells incredible belts with really nice leather-"

"Ignore him" Mako groans, nudging his brother. "He thinks he can buy anything he sees now that he is a mover star"

"A mover star?" Vera asks puzzled, "You are?"

"Sure am" Bolin smirks, "You're looking at Nuktuk- Hero of the South"

Mako rolls his eyes as Vera's eyebrows raise in awe.

"That is really cool" I smile, "I'm sure you've met a lot of cool people"

"Sure have" Bolin bragged, "Tons of famous people. Ginger was my co-star, who was totally into me by the way. And I'm best friends with the Avatar-"

"You're best friends with Avatar Korra?" Vera gasps.

Mako sends his brother a sideways look, my eyes wide in surprise.

"What is the Avatar like?" I ask, "I've read a lot about her"

Bolin shrugs, looking at his hands.

"She's cool" He muses, then smacking Mako's shoulder. "He's the one you should ask though, that's his ex-girlfriend"

I almost choke on my drink, eyes wide as I look at Mako.

"Your ex-girlfriend is Avatar Korra?" I exclaim.

Vera chuckles, twirling her spoon in her cup, "Oh boy"

Mako scratches the back of his neck, "We were together once, yes"

Bolin laughs, "He's a humble guy. Korra was head over heels for him. They broke up but then she almost died and forgot and he had to break it off with her again"

I stare at the brothers wide eyed, mouth slightly open as my mind rushes to process what I had learned.

Mako dated the AVATAR? I knew he was out of my league but this.... This was crazy.

Chapter 5

I lay back on my bed, nerves pounding as I feel the mattress dip beside me. I sigh, eyes squeezing shut in frustration.

"I'm sure it's not a big deal" Vera reasons, "They broke up a while ago according to his brother"

I sit up, distraught "He still dated her! How can I compete with the avatar?!"

"You don't, you just be yourself" Vera says softly, "It's clear Mako is interested in you, I could see him blushing from across the table."

I sigh, looking down at my fingers.

"I guess you're right" I mumble, "I'm just insecure"

Vera pats my shoulder, "It happens to the best of us, but just be yourself and I know it'll work out"

I give her a small smile, reaching in for a hug. After a few moments we pull apart, Vera groaning.

"My head is killing me" she complains, "I'm going to have Bo do a treatment"

She gets up and leaves, I follow and watch her duck into Bo's room.

A few minutes later Vera is lying on the couch, a bowl of water beside us as Bo sits down.

"How was school?" I ask, watching her gather water with her hands.

"It was fine" She says, "Everyone kept asking me questions"

I watch as Bo bends the water, the droplets swirling in the air as she moves them toward Vera's head. Bo flicks her fingers and the water swirls, lying on Vera's temples before the water began to glow.

Bo was a naturally gifted healer, something she got from our mother. She was the only daughter to have waterbending, so naturally she got the most attention with her training. I watch as Bo does her treatment, letting the water rest on Vera's head. Her frown soon relaxes, the pain leaving Vera's head.

"You're getting good at that" Vera said after a while, sitting up.

"I'm the best there is" Bo grinned, moving the droplets of water in the air to play. "The elders at the Southern Water Tribe say I'm a prodigy"

Bo had amazing bending abilities, but lacked when it came to being humble.

I snort, watching her play around with the water when the phone rings.

"Elena!" My dad calls from the other room, "It's for you!"

I sit up and grab the phone, holding it to my ear.

"Hello?"

"Hey, it's Mako"

I smile, "Hey! How are you?"

"I'm well" He replies, his voice charming. "I was wondering if you wanted to hang out tonight. Bolin and I were going to this pro-bender match at the arena. He has a private viewing box with some of his castmates"

"Oh!" I say excitedly, "That sounds great!"

"Cool." Mako replies, I could hear the smile in his voice. "I'll pick you up around 8"

After exchanging farewells, I sat the phone back on the hook. I have so much to do! I had no idea what I was going to wear, nor any clue about the rules of Pro-bending. Let the work begin.

"This says casual, but still classy" Vera states, holding up a white sundress.

"Isn't it a little too casual?" I wince, "Ginger and a bunch of Bolin's mover friends are going to be sitting with us."

Vera nods, looking back to her closet. I sit on the edge of her bed, watching her flick through hangers.

"What about this?" She says, holding up a red dress. The fabric was heavy but elegant, the edges styled with a golden outline.

"It's beautiful" I admire, "But isn't that the dress Iroh...."

"You can have it" Vera presses, tossing the garment on the bed. "I don't want it anymore."

I press my lips together, cursing myself for bringing him up. The dress was one of Vera's favorites when we were in the Fire Nation. She had gotten it with Iroh when they had dinner in the palace. I knew the dress held a lot of memories for her, but perhaps it was time to change the story.

"I'll take good care of it" I smile, standing from the mattress. "Can you help me with my hair?"

"Sure" Vera smiled, stepping toward her vanity.

We sit in silence, the music flowing from the record player on her bed side table as I watch her curl the ends of my hair. After a few minutes Bo came in, legs dangling off the side of the bed as she watched us.

"You look fancy" She giggled, snacking on a sleeve of cookies. "It's weird"

"I'll take that as a compliment" I laugh, moving my head from side to side as I watch the curls in my hair bounce. "It looks great, Vera"

"I think so too" Vera agrees, "My new curler is from Varrick Industries, it was loads better than my old one"

After my hair was sprayed down I got dressed and let Vera apply a thin layer of makeup, and before I knew it I was ready to go.

My stomach was erupting into butterflies as I studied myself in the mirror. I hardly even recognized myself, but I felt beautiful.

"It's almost 8" I huffed, smoothing the fabric of my dress down.

"Don't worry too much" Vera smiled, "Mako is head over heels for you, just be yourself"

"And don't forget to check your teeth for food!" Bo teased.

I give them a nervous smile, hugging them both tight before heading downstairs. After a quick smile to the doorman, I step out to the street to see Mako waiting against his police vehicle, a smile on his face.

"Wow" He smiles, "You look great"

"Thank you" I blush, "So do you"

He was dressed in a grey outfit, accents of red on the sleeves and collar. His hair was in his usual style, but I could tell he put a little gel in. Before I knew it we were on our way to the arena, a crowd of people lining the outside.

Mako parks, taking the key out before he turns to me.

"Ready?" He asks.

"Ready" I smile.

Let the game begin. Literally.

The private suite was incredible. Glass windows lined the wall as a door lead out to more seats that were in the arena. Food lined the walls as soft music played. People stood around, mingling and laughing as I made my way through the crowd with Mako.

Glasses of sparkling juices were handed to us, my fingers balancing the cup as we moved to step out on the balcony. The arena was huge, seats lining the giant walls as a pool of water sat in the middle with a platform in the center. People were taking their seats as the announcer's voice echoed around us.

Standing on the balcony was Bolin, a plate of snacks in his hands as he spoke to a black haired woman I didn't recognize.

"Bro" Mako grinned, patting his back.

"Hello Mako" Bolin enthused, "Lovely to see, Elena"

"Hi, thank you for having me" I smile, "This is incredible"

"Isn't it cool?" Bolin squealed, "The food is fantastic!"

Mako rolled his eyes, turning to the woman.

"Elena, this is my friend Asami Sato" He says, motioning to the woman. "Asami, this is Elena Shen. The daughter of Mr. and Mrs. Shen"

"Oh right" She smirked, "The girl you haven't been able to shut up about"

My cheeks flushed, noticing Mako's eyes widen.

"Hi, it's great to meet you" She smiled, giving me a quick hug.

"Nice to meet you as well" I say.

Asami was tall, her figure slim. She had long raven black hair and piercing green eyes. Her looks reminded me a lot of Vera's. Her nature was calm, she gave off an intelligent vibe.

"How are you liking Republic City?" She asked, glass between her fingers. "I hope the smell of sewage isn't bothering you too much"

I let out a light laugh, "No, not much" I shake my head, "Although it was hard to get used to at first"

Mako then claps his hands, bringing everyone's attention to him.

"I'm going to get some snacks. Anyone want anything?" He asks.

"I'll take whatever Bolin had" Asami says.

I shake my head, Mako turning to leave. I look back, both Bolin and Asami staring at me.

"Has he made a move yet?" Bolin says excitedly.

I open my mouth, thrown off guard by the question.

"He's never been so shy around a girl before" Asami chuckles, "He's got it bad"

"Oh... I-" I stutter, hand scratching the back of my neck. "I didn't know-"

"Sometimes it takes him a while to come to terms with his feelings" Bolin explains, "Don't hold it against him, he has a hard exterior"

I laugh, nodding my head. "That's good to know"

We stand and chat for a few moments about the upcoming match. Mako returns with plates of food while we mingle. I look around the room, the faces of actors familiar to me as I notice Ginger and a few others in the room.

After a few minutes I feel something soft touch my feet. I quickly look down to see a dash of red, a tail wagging as I watch a small animal jump onto Bolin and climb up his arm.

"Oh my!" I exclaim in surprise.

"This is Pabu" Bolin smiles, scratching the fire ferret's head. "He likes to run around"

"He's adorable" I compliment, reaching up to pet his head. Pabu hums in approval, rubbing his head up to the palm of my hand.

"He likes you" Mako states.

"Not everyday a world famous fire ferret becomes your friend" I joke, "I saw him on the posters for your mover"

Bolin grins, "He's a ladies man, just like me"

-Mako-

I knew it was weird to stare. My mind kept screaming at me to look away, but I was so drawn to the woman next to me, I couldn't help it. I knew this match was a big deal, and whoever won would make it to the next round of the championship- and normally I would have cared. But not tonight.

I sat beside Elena, our shoulders brushing on the balcony seats as the match began. The sounds of cheering fell silent to my ears as I watched her bright eyes scan the court in front of us.

She was charming, easy to talk to. She fell perfectly in sync with Bolin and Asami- just like I knew she would. Watching her react to the match was more entertaining than the match itself, if I'm being honest.

The rounds flew by, the underdog team advancing to the next match as we stood from our seats.

"That was great!" Elena grinned, "I didn't know pro-bending could be so intense!"

"It's a rough sport" Bolin commented, "Mako and I still have scars from it"

"I didn't know you were a pro-bender" Elena says, eyes connecting with mine.

I just shrug, "It was more for money, not really my passion"

"But we did win the championship a few years ago" Bolin sang.

Her eyes twinkled, enthusiasm clear in her face.

"That is so cool!" she grinned, "I would love to see you guys play"

"Maybe you can play with us" Bolin suggested, "Are you a waterbender?"

Elena shakes her head, "No, only my mother and my sister are benders"

Asami nodded, wrapping her arm over her shoulders, "Nice to have another non-bender around"

Elena smiled, a light laugh coming from her as we walked out of the private room.

We get outside, the sky dark as the clouds block the moon. It was starting to get chilly out, the breeze causing us all to shiver.

I glance at Elena, her arms wrapped around herself as we walk toward the car. I hesitate for a moment, head reeling before I unravel my own red scarf and wrap it around her shoulders.

"It's not much, but it'll help block some of the wind" I said gently.

She smiles, thanking me before wrapping it around her neck.

We say our goodbyes to Bolin and Asami, Elena exchanging quick hugs before we get into my kart. The air cold as I turn to her.

"Did you have fun?" I ask.

"I did" She nods, "Thank you for bringing me, Mako."

I smile, watching her rub her palms together to try and warm up. I chuckle, reaching over and covering her palms with my own. I hear her gasp, heat flowing through my hands over hers to try and warm her up.

"You're so warm," she whispers.

"And you're so cold" I joke in reply.

She laughs, licking her lips nervously before starting again:

"You're friend Asami is great" she comments, "I really like her, and Bolin too of course"

I smile, keeping my hands in place. "They're great, I'm lucky to have them"

"Do you talk to Avatar Korra often?" She asks.

I shrug, looking out the window. "Not as much as I used to" I sigh, "We had a lot going on the last couple of months, and she decided to take a break with the Airbenders. We don't hear from her very often."

Elena frowns, "I'm sorry to hear that" she says, "I heard all the amazing stories and the things you've done."

I shrug again, suddenly shy.

"We're all a team" I explain, "We help each other out"

The sound of cars honking breaks our mood, and I suddenly realize we have to leave. I take my hands away from hers, starting the car and going onto the road. The radio is fuzzing, a jazz song playing as we sit in comfortable silence.

After a few blocks I pull up to her building on the Upper East Side, turning the car off and sliding out. I open the door for her, a smile on her face as we greet the door man and ride up to the 20th level.

"So, do you want to go to the next match with me?" I ask, glancing at her in the elevator.

"Of course!" She beams, "I think I found a new hobby!"

I laugh, the bell ringing and the doors opening. We step out, moving down the hallway. Suddenly our moods shift, a frown crossing my lips as we see her apartment door wide open.

Elena rushes over, standing in the doorway as a gasp escaped her lips. I run over, eyes widening at the sight. Her living room was completely trashed, pillows ripped, paintings fallen. It looked like someone had broken it and torn the place apart.

This wasn't good.

Chapter 6

Everything was happening in slow motion, my head spinning as I stepped into my home. The carpet was ruined, glass shattered as I looked around. Tears pooled in my eyes as I looked at my piano, the keys smashed and wires torn. It was ruined.

I felt a sob come out, my hand cupping my face as I looked around.

"Dad!" I cry, moving around the room. "Vera!"

Mako was behind me, looking at the damage as I looked in each room.

"Bo!" I yell, "Dad!"

"Dr. Shen!" Mako echos, peeking through doors and into rooms. Everything was trashed, my vanity smashed, drawers thrown around the room. All of my possessions were thrown around and crushed.

Tears rolled down my cheeks as I looked at Mako. "They're gone"

He looks at me, his face serious as he turns and goes back to the parlor.

I follow, arms hugging myself as I watch him pick up the telephone.

"The wires have been cut" He announces, "Stay with me"

I sniff, following him as we head back down to the lobby of my building. Mako rushes to his police kart, leaning over the seat to radio the station. I stand in the middle of the sidewalk, nerves pumping as he comes back to me.

"Chief Beifong is coming with some other officers" He says, "I'm going to call Bolin and have him come and take you to a hotel"

"No" I rush, "No, I want to stay and help find my family"

"Elena" Mako says sternly, "This is crime scene, you could be in danger"

"All the more reason to stay with you" I argue.

I had no idea what was going on. My head was spinning, tears spilling out of my eyes. My family was missing. My dad, Vera, and Bo. I had no idea what could have happened. I don't know if they are safe, or hurt.

Mako runs a hand through his hair, looking around.

"We'll wait until the chief gets here and we'll figure something out"

I swallow hard, following Mako back up to my ruined apartment. I kneel down, picking up the torn pieces of sheet music and cry, my head hanging low. I feel the Mako's warm touch on my shoulder, his hand soothing as I weep.

"What if something bad happened?" I sob, looking up at him with blurred eyes. "What is going to happen?"

"We'll find them" Mako promises, "I'll find them"

A knock on the door makes us look up, Mako answering as Chief Beifong enters followed by a team of officers. Her eyes were serious, her gaze narrow as she studied the room.

"Elena" she says, helping me stand. "What happened before you left?"

"I was getting ready to go to the match. My sisters were with me and my father was here. I left at 8" I explain, "I don't know of anyone else coming over tonight"

She nods, turning to an officer: "I want evidence taken from every room. Radio every officer in the city and tell them to start patrolling, not a single vehicle goes by without being checked."

The officers nod, moving around the room as I sniff.

"Elena, I'm afraid you can't stay here so we are going to have to put you in a hotel room-"

"She can stay with me"

Our eyes turn to Mako, his hand raised in the air as he looks between me and the chief.

"She can stay with me, she'll be safe." Mako repeats.

Beifong nods, hands on her hips as she turns to me.

"I trust Mako, you'll be safe there" She says, "Mako, take her home."

He nods, leading me out of the parlor and into the hallway. I turn and glance at my home one last time, officers moving around the room looking for evidence. With a sigh I walk forward, my steps in sync with Mako.

In the elevator I turn to him, lip quivering in sadness.

He pulls me into his arms, his chin resting on my head as I feel his arms wrap around me in a warm hug. I let out a sob, my tears soaking into his shirt.

"I'm so scared," I cry.

I hear him whisper reassuring things, his hand rubbing my back as the door opens. With puffy eyes I let him take my hand in his and led me out and back into his car. I slide in, letting him close the door behind me and watch as he goes to the drivers side.

My hands shake slightly, nerves pumping through me as we pull away. Tears run down my cheeks as I watch my building go by, the feeling of a warm hand on top of mine calming me slightly.

After a few minutes in the car we pull up to a 4 story building. Mako helps me out, unlocking the door and leading us up a flight of stairs and down a dimly lit hallway. He unlocks it and pushes the door open, a small cozy apartment meeting my eyes.

It was clean, just as I would have thought. The couch was tan, the fireplace sitting on the side as the small kitchen sat on the other. A few windows faced the street, a door leading into the bedroom as another went into the washroom.

Mako tosses his key on the table, clicking on the lights. "Kitchen is there, and that room is my bedroom."

I nod, sliding off my shoes and stepping onto the wooden floor.

I followed him into his bedroom, a bed sat in the middle of the room beside a small table. A dresser sat on the other side, a shelf full of books and photos hovering above. I watch Mako open a drawer, a shirt in his hands.

"I don't have anything smaller" He says, "But for now, this is what you can sleep in"

I thank him, looking around the room.

"I'll sleep on the couch" He states. I open my mouth to protest but he stops me, "I insist. You've been through enough tonight- the last thing you need is a back ache"

I nod, looking down as I feel tears roll down my face.

"I'll make you some tea"

The door closes and I'm left alone. Hazily I step into the washroom, using the small basin to wash my makeup off and change into Mako's shirt. The fabric was soft and smelled like him. The length hitting just down my thighs.

I look at myself in the mirror, my eyes red and puffy as my cheeks were flushed red. I felt awful. I don't know how I'm going to sleep tonight, but the wave of emotions both woke me up and exhausted me.

"Elena"

I open the door, Mako waiting on the side with a small cup of tea.

"Bolin told me it's good when I can't sleep" He states, "I guess it relaxes you"

I take it, the cup warm between my fingers as I sip it.

"Thank you" I say, my voice rough. "It's delicious"

"If you need anything, I'll be outside" Mako tells me, "Don't hesitate to call for me"

I nod, watching him step out and close the door. I sit on the bed, the blankets soft as I sigh. I drink the tea, letting the heat warm my belly before crawling under the covers and thankfully finding sleep.

The next morning I blink awake, the beams of sun shining into my eyes as I roll onto my back. At first I'm confused, the stone ceiling was different from the one in my room. Then reality settles in, the pit in my stomach returning.

I sigh, mind flashing through the events of the night before. My body felt tired, even after a whole night of sleep I still felt exhausted.

The sound of voices perks my attention, my legs sliding off the bed as I step out into the main living space. Sat at the table was Asami, Bolin leaning against the stone counter in the kitchen. Their conversation pauses when they see me, my footsteps alerting them.

"Morning" Asami says sweetly, her face cheerful. "We cooked you break-fast"

"Thanks" I say, shuffling to sit across from her, "But I'm not sure I have much of an appetite"

She nods, mouth turning into a sympathetic smile.

I look around, the fire crackling as a blanket was thrown lazily across the couch.

"Mako went down to the station," Bolin says, as if he was reading my mind. "He wanted us to keep you company"

"You guys don't have to do that" I say, guilt flooding over me, "I'm sure you guys are busy-"

"Don't worry about it" Asami presses, "You're one of us now, we are always there for each other"

Her statement warms my heart, a smile spreading across my face as I sit back. Sure, the last 12 hours had been hell, but at least I didn't have to go through it alone.

"Hey, Mako left his scarf" Bolin notices, walking to the couch. "He never leaves without it"

"He let me borrow it last night" I say, eyebrows turning in confusion at their stunned looks. "What?"

"Mako never takes it off" Asami tells me, "ever."

"It belonged to our father" Bolin explains, the red garment in his hands, "It's one of

the only things we have left of our parents. It means the world to him"

"And he let you have it" Asami ethuses.

"Just to borrow" I correct, "I would never want him to give me something so special

to him"

"He never lets anyone wear it" Bolin says, "Not even Asami and Korra"

"It's true" Asami nods to me, "Never once did he let me try it on when we were

together"

"You and Mako dated?" I ask, puzzled.

"Briefly" Asami says, "We are much better as friends"

I nod, biting my lip. Not only did he date the Avatar, but Asami, who is a beautiful

woman I could never compete with.

Silence fills the room, the sound of utensils hitting the plate as Bolin finished his serving of eggs. I walk around the room, arms crossed as I frown.

"Mako hasn't heard anything?" I ask, worry flooding over me.

"No" Asami frowns, "But I'm sure he'll call soon with something"

"I hope" I sigh, "I can't stand just sitting here" I groan.

Bolin nods, setting his now empty plate down before moving into the living space.

"I know what will cheer you up" He says, "Lets listen to some music!"

He clicks on the dark brown radio, the static laced music notes flowing through the room. I nod, sitting back on the couch as he sits down beside me.

The song plays for a few minutes before it's interrupted by the crackling voice of the radio host.

"Good Afternoon, we come to you now with breaking news: Dr Shen and his daughters Vera and Bo have gone missing after a break in of his Upper East Side apartment last night. Republic City police are on the hunt for them but-"

"Let's do something else," Asami says, clicking the radio off. "Anyone up for a game of Pai Sho?"

-Mako-

The sound of broken glass crunches under my boots, my feet stepping around dismembered furniture as I look around the disheveled apartment. I sigh, rubbing the sides of my forehead while I take in the scene around me.

There were tags everywhere, each disturbance noted by a detective as offi-cers look around for any clues. So far, nothing significant has been found. Chief Beifong has been circling all day- directing the investigation and giving out orders. President Raiko had already been notified, his reaction was to be expected. He was outraged- and demanded we find the Doctor and his daughters as soon as possible.

I frown, moving to look at the destroyed piano in front of me. It was smashed, the keys falling off as it looked like someone took a hammer to it. It pained me to see it, I knew how much Elena loved it and how special of an item it was.

Under my boot was a stack of paper, the edges crumpled and ripped, but I somehow recognized the scribbles. I reach down, taking the pieces of paper in my hands and look them over. It was Elena's song she wrote for the charity event coming up.

I lighty fold the papers, sliding them into my jacket pocket before moving on to the next thing to look for clues.

The sun was starting to sink into the night when I left the Shen's apart-ment. My eyes laced with sleep as I unlocked my door and walked in. The living room smelled amazing, the heat of the fire crackling as I noticed a steaming bowl of soup awaiting me on the table.

I smile, shrugging off my jacket and tossing it aside. I happily ate the meal, setting the dirty dish aside before turning to rest on the couch. The door then cracks, Elena stepping out. She was in a white nightgown, her hair wet and going down her shoulders.

"Hey" she greeted, stepping into the room. "How was it?"

"It went well" I say, "We found some things to send to the lab"

"So, they'll find a clue soon?" Elena says hopefully.

I nod, kicking my boots off my feet. "I believe so"

She smiles, sitting back against the cushions.

"I'll sleep here tonight" She says lightly, "We can take turns-"

"Not happening" I say, "It's uncomfortable as hell"

"That's exactly why we should take turns" Elena reasons, "You're the one going to work all day, not me."

I look at her, her green eyes looking back at me. I knew it was the right thing to do- to insist on sleeping here. I couldn't let her sleep on the couch, her back would hurt for days.

"Elena" I sigh

"Mako" She retorts.

"Where did you get the outfit?" I ask, changing the subject.

She looks down, the fabric of her night dress hugging her body.

"Asami brought some clothes over" She explains, "Your clothes are nice, but maybe not my size"

I laugh, sitting back. "Are you implying something?" I smirk.

Her eyes widen, expression changing into shock.

"No! Of course not" she defends, I meet her worried eyes with a laugh.

"I was only joking, Elena" I smile, "It looks nice on you"

She blushes, looking down at her lap.

"Thank you, Mako" she says sweetly, "For everything"

I open my mouth to reply, but she cuts me off with her words:

"I know it's your duty, and I know you are an honorable man- but you have been so kind to me. I know I can trust you and in a time like this, that means everything"

"You're welcome" I respond, tone serious, "Elena, I would do anything for you"

The words run out of my mouth before I can stop, both of our eyes widening at my statement. Even though it was intense, and carried a lot of weight- it was true. Elena Shen was someone I would do anything for.

And that is exactly what I planned to do.

Chapter 7

I blink awake, the familiar beams of light shining into my eyes as I roll over. I'm once again met with the warmth of Mako's bed. The fabric feels soft against my skin as I wake up. I hear the sound of music flowing from the living room, the hissing of a kettle adding to the noise.

I roll out of bed, stretching my arms as I open the bedroom door. Bolin stands in the kitchen, two cups before him as he hums a tune along with the radio.

"Morning" I say, sliding into a seat.

"Goooood morning" He chirps, "Rest well?"

"I did" I nod, "How long have you been here?"

Bolin simply shrugs, the single curl on his forehead bouncing as he moves.

"Not long, an hour?"

I frown, "I was hoping to go with Mako to the station. I feel weird sitting around not helping"

"It's safer if you stay hidden," Bolin states, picking up the kettle and pouring warm cups of tea. "He told me to make sure you don't go anywhere alone"

I nod, taking the cup in my fingers.

"Still" I whine, "I want to help"

"I know" Bolin nods, sipping from the steaming cup. "But trust me, we've done crazier things. Mako usually knows what's best"

"Tell me about your adventures" I say, curiosity rolling through me, "The newspapers never do the story justice"

Bolin leans back against the counter, gaze switching out the window.

"Where do I even begin?" He says dreamily, "We fought Amon, who was this crazy cult leader who tried to destroy all benders. But it turned out he was a bender himself. And then there was the evil spirit that tried to take over the world, but we managed to get that under control too"

"Wow" I say, swallowing a dose of the warm peach tea, "You've done amazing things"

"I'm sure you've done cool stuff too" Bolin reasons, "Haven't you been all over the world?"

I shrug, "We moved around a lot, my parents worked with a lot of world leaders."

"So you've met the Earth queen and Fire Lord Izumi" Bolin asks.

I nod, "We lived in Ba Sing Se when I was young, I don't remember much. But we spent about 4 years in the Fire Nation. My parents are close friends with Fire Lord Zuko"

"Wow" Bolin whistles, "What was the Fire Nation like?"

"Really cool" I grin, "The palace is really extravagant, lots of gold and fancy decorations"

"I would like to go there someday" Bolin says, "But even more so the Earth Kingdom"

"Ba Sing Se is large, very busy" I confess, "Omashu is really neat too"

"There's a really good Earth Kingdom themed restaurant a few blocks away" Bolin tells me, "When you're off house arrest we should go"

"That sounds great" I smile.

A knock on the door makes us turn, Bolin getting up and opening the oak door. Two men stand on the other side, a large package behind them.

"We have a delivery here for Mako?" One man says.

"Sure" Bolin says, waving them in.

I watch as the men carry a large box inside, Bolin helping move a bookcase over to make room. After a few papers are given and signed, Bolin closes the door. He turns to face me, his expression excited.

"Open it!" He grins

"What is it?" I ask, touching the top of the giant package.

"Just open it!" He repeats.

I laugh, untying the rope holding the box together. Under the brown boxing was a thin layer of fabric. I remove it to find a smooth black surface. My heart starts to beat, quickly removing the rest of the packaging to reveal a small piano.

The keys were bright, the surface smooth and flat as it sits against the wall. Tears begin to form, my fingers moving over the top.

"Oh my" I sigh happily, "This is amazing"

"It was all Mako" Bolin says from behind me, "Pretty cool, huh?"

"It's beautiful," I gasp.

I move the bench out and sit down, my fingers pressing on a few keys. The notes were delightful, my heart swelling at the new item. I can't believe Mako thought of this.

"It's tuned" I state in awe. "How did he do this?"

"We all pitched in" Bolin says, hands shoved in his pockets. "We thought it would help you feel better, since you can't go to the conservatory to practice"

"Thank you" I smile, "It's lovely"

I spent hours at the bench, the piano soothing my nerves. I play around with some chords, absentmindedly playing old tunes as Bolin sits on the couch and watches. Time seemed to fly by, my mind not wondering any farther than from the instrument at my fingertips.

Soon the door opens, Mako stepping in with a small smile. I turn, rushing up from my place at the piano and wrap him up in a big hug.

"Thank you so much" I say into his neck, his scent calming. "It's amazing"

"I'm glad you like it" Mako says, hands on my back as he returns the embrace. "I wasn't sure if I ordered the right thing"

"It's perfect," I grin, stepping back. "I can teach you more chords!"

Bolin snorts, "Mako has a much music ability as he does Earthbending"

I let out a laugh, Mako's eyebrows pulling together.

"Don't you have to be at the studio making movers or something?" He teases back.

Bolin gives him a cheeky smile, grabbing his coat and wishing us farewell, closing the door promptly behind him.

"Have you heard anything from my mother?" I ask, standing from the piano.

"Not yet" Mako says, moving around the kitchen, "We sent out a notice to all the villages, last we heard she was with a tribe in the mountains. Whenever she comes into a village we should be able to get her home"

I nod, biting my lip in thought.

Mako's eyes connect with mine, my face serious. I knew he could read my expression and could tell I was worried.

"She's gonna be fine, Elena" he states, stepping toward me. "So is the rest of your family"

I sigh, nodding as my eyes lock with the floor. "I just feel so useless sitting around here all day. That's my family, I should be doing something"

"You're doing exactly what you should be doing," Mako says, his voice stern. "The most important thing is for you to take care of yourself, getting yourself into trouble won't help them"

I nod. I knew he was right, but even with the logic laid out in front of me- it was still hard to accept. Mako moves around the kitchen, the hissing of a kettle ringing around the small apartment as he prepares dinner.

We stand side by side, Mako flipping meat in the skillet as I chop up various vegetables and steam rice. Within a few minutes we are sitting at the small table, the pillow under me soft to the touch as we dig into our meal.

"What is your favorite food?" I ask, picking up a steamed carrot with my chopsticks.

"Easy: dumplings" Mako replies mindlessly. "My mother used to make them when I was little. Her and I would stuff them and fold them, it was fun."

"Is that how you learned to cook?" I ask, "From your mother?"

Mako nods gently, "I didn't have a lot of time to learn with her, but I picked up a few things from watching her."

"That's so sweet" I smile, noting the faint smile on his face. "We didn't spend a lot of time cooking when I was growing up"

Mako looks up at me, a cup of tea between his fingers. "How so?"

I shrug, "My parents were busy working, and with their jobs we travelled a lot. Most of the time we were staying as guests so we didn't have to make our own food"

"It's neat you got to stay in cool places, though" Mako muses, I nod gently.

"It had its moments" I say, "But I never really got to have a home. We were always staying in other people's houses. I didn't get to have my own room, it was always a guest room. It was hard growing up and getting comfortable in one place then having to change everything and do it all again in a new place."

"I can imagine" Mako nods, his golden eyes looking back at me. "Where was your favorite place?"

I think for a moment, my mind reviewing memories over my childhood. Between all the places we lived, I had the best time in the Fire Nation.

"Fire Nation" I announce, "I liked the climate, leaving that and going to the Water Tribe was a hard adjustment"

"And you lived in the capital?"

I nod, "The palace- yes. I loved watching the firebenders train, I was always fascinated by it"

Mako smirks, a playful expression on his lips, "Firebending is pretty cool, huh?"

I roll my eyes playfully, a grin spreading on my face.

"Fire Lord Zuko would sometimes battle against my sister Bo, he would always let her win" I laugh.

The smile on my face slowly fades, my laughter dying out as the memories of my childhood are replaced by the sobering reality I was in. My family was gone.

Mako notices, his fingers dropping the chopsticks and his palm resting on top of my hand. I look up at him, not noticing the blurriness from my tears.

"It's going to be alright, Elena" He reassures me, "I promise."

Chapter 8

Mako-

The smell of freshly brewed coffee and ink was all too familiar as I pushed open the office doors. The station was busy, agents rushing around with papers and photos as I weaved my way through the hustle and bustle and into Chief Beifong's office.

I came in a hurry, my radio buzzing early in the morning. I was told to get to the station as fast as possible, thus my shoes were half tied and my shirt untucked as I plop down in the chair.

"Mako" Chief nods, walking into the room. A few officer's followed, the bags under their eyes telling me it had been a long night. "We have bad news"

I frown, my stomach sinking.

"Elena's mother is missing" Lin frowns, "We got a radio call in the night from a village outside Omashu. Sakura Shen's camp was raided, her and her team are missing"

I sigh, fingers pinching the bridge of my nose in frustration. Elena had been counting on her mother getting here, and now she was missing along with everyone else.

"We don't have any leads?" I say, frustrated.

Chief shakes her head, hands leaning on the desk.

"I'm thinking about going there to investigate, I think it would be best if you came along. I need my best officer's with me"

"I'm in" I announced, standing from my seat. "I can ask Bolin and Asami to stay with Elena"

She nods, dark eyes connecting with mine, "You need to tell her, Mako"

"I know" I sigh, hand running through my hair, "I will"

"We leave in 4 hours"

I nod, exiting the office and making my way back out of the station. This wasn't going to be easy.

After a few minutes I'm met with the outside of my apartment building, my heart pounding as I walk past the doors and up the stairs. I hate this. I hate being the one to deliver bad news.

I open the door, music filling the room as Elena sits at the piano. At first she didn't even see me walk in. Her eyes cast on the wall as her fingers slide up and down the keys. Her hair was down, flowing down her shoulders. A white silk shirt sat on her body, the sleeves long and flowing as she moved her fingers up and down the piano. She looked peaceful, calm. I didn't want to be the thunderstorm to rain on her good mood.

"Elena" I said, watching her fingers halt as the music stopped.

"You're home early" she noted, a small pressed to her lips, "Want some Jasmine tea?"

"N-no, no thank you" I hesitate, stepping forward. "Elena, something happened"

Her smile falls, green eyes widening. I could see the wave of anxiety hit her, and it made me feel sick.

"The station received a radio call from a village outside Omashu, your mother's camp was raided and she and her team are missing" I say, watching her worry turn to sorrow.

Within seconds she is on the ground, knees buckling as sobs echo around my apartment. I rush to her, bending down to place a warm hand on her shoulder. I move my hand steadily up and down her shaking frame, my heart pulling at the sound of her crying.

Watching her in this state made me feel sick. There was no way I could leave her to go with Chief to Omashu. How could I? I need to be here, with her. I could never leave.

After a few minutes she sets up, legs sprawled out on the floor as she sniffs. Her eyes and nose were red, the puffiness of her eyes making me hurt even more. I hated seeing her sad.

"It's going to be okay" I assured her, eyes staring into her own.

She kept her mouth closed, eyes tamed on her hands.

"I can't do this anymore, Mako" she says, voice husky and dry from crying. "I can't sit here and do nothing anymore"

"Elena-" I lecture.

"No" She interrupts, standing abruptly. "I have no one left, I don't even know if they are alive. I'm sick of sitting here like a damsel in distress. It's time I do something"

"Elena" I begin, standing straight, "You can't act irrationally, this is life or death"

"You think I don't know that?" She cries, eyebrows pulled together in anger. "That is exactly why I have to go out and try."

"But you could get hurt" I say, begging her to listen to my voice of reason.

It fell numb to her ears, her feet carrying her to the door.

"Elena, please!"

"I'm not sitting here another day and watching the people I love get taken away" She yells, hands going to pull her long hair into a ponytail with an elastic band. "I'm going to talk to Chief Beifong"

I sigh, hands rubbing my face in frustration.

"Then, at least let me go with you"

"Will you try and stop me?" She quizzes, eyebrow raised in question.

"No" I sigh, slipping my shoes on. "I won't"

-Elena-

I push the double doors of the station, officers moving around like ants in a colony. I don't even stop to greet them as I walk straight through the chaos and into the Chief's office.

Lin Beifong looks up, standing quickly as I stand disheveled in the doorway. I feel Mako stop a few steps behind me, my chest heaving.

"Elena" she greets.

"I want in" I say, "I want to help find my family"

"That isn't a good idea-"

I hold my hand up, irritation washing over me. "I've heard this before, and no, I'm not going to listen. What can I do to help get my family back?"

Lin looks behind me, her eyes locking with Mako before glancing back at me. She turns, picking up a paper before walking around her desk and handing it to me.

"I radioed Tenzin and his family, they should return here with the Avatar in a few days. When she returns she will be leading a group of officers on a mission to investigate your mother's campsite near Omashu."

"What can we do here, while she is gone?" I ask, "There must be something I can do from Republic City"

She nods, fingers tapping her chin. "There was something I had in mind"

I hear Mako inhale sharply, my attention snapping back to the Chief.

"Your concert at the conservatory is in a few weeks. It's a very high profile event with a lot of attention and publicity. We could use your performance as bait to try and catch whoever has been after your family"

"Absolutely not," Mako snaps, stepping forward. "We aren't going to use her as a sitting duck, it is too dangerous"

"I'll do it," I say, not even bothering to think it over.

This was the first chance we'd get to try and catch the culprit. I'm not letting this opportunity pass by. Mako groans, turning and leaving with a slam of the door. I look back to Lin Biefong, a serious expression on her face.

"I assure you, you will be safe" She promises.

I nod, crossing my arms over my chest. This should be interesting.

That night I'm left with a bowl of noodles and an empty apartment. The ride back home was quiet, Mako keeping to himself. We arrived home and he excused himself, making up an excuse to leave before disappearing.

I sat in front of the fire, hair freshly brushed as I stared into the flames.

I was nervous. Nervous for my family, for this plan, and nervous something could go horribly wrong. My gut told me to be strong, but my brain kept voicing its doubts. I trusted Mako and Chief Beifong, but they were only human. They could only do so much.

The flames swirl in front of me, the crackling of wood reminding me of my time in the Fire Nation. Our family suite had a giant fireplace, the golden crest of the Fire Lord hung high. The smell of burnt wood reminded me of all the nights we'd spent in front of the fire, playing Pai Sho and laughing.

My heart sank, the memories melancholy to me now.

An idea then rang in my mind, my body jumping up and rushing to grab a slip of paper and a pen. Quickly, I sit on my knees and scribble the name, my pen flying across the page.

Iroh,

I hope this letter finds you well. I am writing to you because I am in need of your help. As you may know, my family has been taken. So far, we have no leads on the suspects, and I fear our time might be running out. I am asking for your assistance in this matter, and pray the United Forces and the Fire Nation might be able to spare some soldiers to aid in the investigation.

I know Vera means a lot to you, as she does to me. If not for me, for her.

I am awaiting your response eagerly.

Take care,

Elena Shen

Chapter 9

I roll onto my side, the beams of moonlight illuminating the room as I blink. The sound of shuffling causes me to stir, my body sitting up as I look around the room in confusion. Light shines from under the door, the shuffling of steps echoing as I peel off my blanket and step to the door.

I open it and see Mako pacing, his boxers hanging on his hips as his face carries a frown. I lean against the door frame, arms folded as I watch him.

"You're going to ruin the floor, you know"

He turns, eyes wide in surprise.

"I'm sorry, did I wake you?"

I shake my head, stepping forward, "How long have you been awake?"

He shrugs, fingers scratching the back of his neck, "All night, I think"

I frown, "Do you want some Chamomile tea?"

"No" He shakes his head, plopping onto the couch. "I'll be alright"

I scoff, sitting down beside him, "I don't think you'll ever be alright, Mako. You worry yourself too much"

He shrugs, fingers folding in front of him.

"Perhaps"

I look at him, the moonlight faintly showing his worried expression. His lips were turned into a frown, worry lines prominent on his forehead. The faint sound of rain against the window begins to ring around the room.

"Is this about the investigation?" I whisper, "About me joining?"

"How could it not be?" He snaps, turning to look at me. "The last thing I want is for you to be used as bait. For you to sit on a stage defenseless as we wait for these criminals to come."

"It's going to help my family" I press, "I have to do this"

"No, you don't" He argues, "You could stay here, stay safe and let me do this. I can do this."

"I know you can. I don't doubt you" I say, eyes looking at him. The wind whips, rain hitting the window harshly as the moonlight fades away. "I just need to do this, I need to help."

He sighs, "I know, I understand." He says, turning back to face the front. "I just can't stand the thought of you in danger."

"I'll be alright" I say delicately, "You'll be there right beside me"

He turns, our shoulders brushing. The memory of us sitting at the piano at the conservatory flashes in my mind, the feeling of his touch sending electricity through my body.

"I won't ever leave your side" He whispers, honey colored eyes never leaving mine. "I'll do anything to protect you"

"I trust you" I whisper, feeling his face come closer to mine.

"Show me" He says, his voice barely audible, "Show me how much you trust me"

Before I could even think, his lips connect with mine, his warm palm cupping my chin as our lips move against each other. My fingers rest on his shoulder, the feeling of his fingers in my hair making my heart swirl.

I feel his hands radiate heat, the temperature in the room rising as we embrace. Our kisses deepen, my lips parting as he slides a hand to hold my waist. My mind was reeling, excitement flowing through me as we kiss.

A few minutes later we pull apart, his forehead resting against mine. I feel our chest heaving together, his hand resting on the side of my face as my fingers play with the fabric of his shirt resting on his shoulder.

"Do you feel better now?" I muse, laughing gently.

He laughs lightly in return, licking his lips. "I do, yeah"

I smile, exhaling happily. "I've been waiting on you to kiss me"

He pulls his head away, eyes looking into mine with a curious expression. "Is that so?"

I nod, biting my lip playfully, "I did, it took you long enough"

Mako chuckles, hand slipping from my face to intertwine with my fingers.

"I think it's time I head to bed" He says softly, I nod. Standing up from the couch. A smile plays on my lips, the feeling of contentment settling into my body. I had waited for him to kiss me for so long, and even in the storm we were enduring, it was nice to have a small break to bask in the sun.

Clothes were everywhere, a maid standing with a tray of refreshments as I sat on the small loveseat. The double doors were open, articles of clothing were tossed around as I watched Asami do her magic. Today I was visiting her house and attempting to decide on a gown for the Benefit. Asami assured me she would have some options, but I had no idea she had an entire store in her closet.

"What do you think about this one?" She asks, hair neatly pinned back as she holds up a gold colored dress in front of me.

"It's pretty" I admire, "But I don't think gold is my color"

Asami scoffs, a playful look in her eye. "You are overthinking it. Try it on!"

I take the dress, the hanger balancing between my fingers as I step to the side. This was the tenth dress I'd tried on today, and I was beginning to loathe formal attire.

I step back into her line of sight, the dress hanging on my body. It didn't look terrible, but everything I had worn today just didn't feel right.

"I think it's pretty" Asami comments, "Gold looks great on you!"

I give her a small, thin lined smile, moving to stand beside her. I move my fingers through the row of dresses, my eyes catching a deep red dress in the very back.

"You should try that one on" Asami says, "That is one of my favorites"

"Are you sure?" I say shyly, "Red is an intense color, I don't know if I can pull it off"

Asami rolls her eyes, grabbing me by the shoulders and steering me toward the screen divider. "Less talking- more trying the dress on!"

I shrug off the gold one and bring the red one to my body. It was a deep red, almost the color of blood. It was long, the skirt flowing around me as the top clings tightly to my chest. I zipped it up, stepping out from behind the screen to be met with a gasp.

"It's perfect!" Asami grins, "You are wearing that!"

I blush, moving to stand in front of the full length mirror on the wall. The color made my skin look pale, the red silky fabric a stark contrast to my brown hair. The sleeves fell to my wrists, the neckline resting at my collarbones.

"I love it" I say, my eyes never leaving my figure in the mirror.

"Mako is going to love it" Asami notes, a mischievous look on her face.

"You think so?" I ask softly, cheeks burning red. Memories of last night flash in my mind, the feeling of his lips against mine still fresh in my memory.

"You look like a tomato" Asami teases, "You're almost redder than the dress!"

"Oh please" I defend, stepping away from the mirror. "I get flushed easily"

"I'm sure" Asami chuckles, sitting on the loveseat. "How are things going with Mako, anyway?"

"It's going well" I smile, moving behind the screen divider. My fingers find the zipper, as I start to change back into my regular clothes. "I think he likes me"

"You think?" She snorts, "He's head over heels for you"

I nod, slipping on my shirt and pants. With a quick glance in the mirror I step out, moving to sit beside Asami with a sigh.

"I'm just worried I'll mess it up" I confess, eyes cast to the ground. "I've never dated anyone before."

"Just be yourself" Asami smiles, "All you have to do is act natural"

I nod, taking in her advice. A small pang in my heart aches, hearing her quote Vera. In that moment I think of my older sister and how much I miss her. It was nice having Asami around, but no one will ever be able to compare to Vera.

"Thank you, Asami" I say, "You've been a great friend"

"Of course" she waves it off, "I'll get the dress steamed and sent to Mako's"

"Perfect" I stand, "I have to head down to the station for a meeting. I'll see you later"

The walls of the conference room were filled with papers and photos, notes clipped to the wall as evidence was sprawled around. Part of me was happy to see the mess, it showed just how hard they were working to get this solved. But another avoided it, the piercing eyes of my loved ones made me feel sad.

' I sit down, the bamboo seat covered by a pillow as I look at the crowd. Chief Beifong was on the end, papers stacked in front of her as officers sat on both sides. A folder is passed to me, notes scribbled out as I flip through the pages.

"This is the plan for the charity benefit" Lin tells me, "Look it over, let me know if you have any questions."

I nod, reading the first few lines before a knock on the door makes us all look up.

"Pardon me" A young woman officer says, peeking her head in the room, "There is a Mr. Nakamura outside."

My eyes widen, jumping from my seat as I move around the table. The chief says something I ignore, my feet carrying me out of the conference room and into the main offices. Sitting in the chair was a man with straight black hair, his clothes a dark green as his bangs fell over his eyes.

I smile, stepping in front of him.

"Tadashi?"

He looks up, smiles crossing his young face as he stands.

"Elena!" He grins, "Thank the spirits you are okay, I came as quickly as I could"

His arms wrap around me in a tight hug, his forest scent familiar.

"I can't believe you are here!" I say, stepping back. "I'm in shock!"

"My father is on his way, he got held up in Ba Sing Se." Tadashi explains, "Have they heard anything about your family?"

"Nothing yet, but we're trying" I frown, "A few pieces of evidence are being examined and Avatar Korra is on her way to lead a search party near Omashu"

Tadashi nods, hands sitting on his hips.

"Well, I'm here. How can I help?"

I smile, happy to see a familiar face as I reach up and pull him into another hug. My arms wrap around his neck, my nose nuzzled into his neck. His palms rest on my back, pulling me close.

A cough makes us turn and pull apart, a confused looking Mako standing before us.

"Did I miss something?"

Chapter 10

"And then I said, 'What does it look like? Metal?"

Everyone at the table erupts into laughter, a charmed smile sitting on Tadashi's lips as we sit. Everyone was gathered at Mako's, a steaming bowl of noodles in front of us as we gathered. It's Tadashi's first night in Republic City, and I convinced Mako to let me host a welcoming dinner.

Bolin, Asami, and Mako sat on one side, while I sat beside my old friend on the other. It felt good to see him, to talk about old times and to enjoy the company of friends. For a few hours my nerves didn't keep me from enjoying myself.

"So, how do you and Elena know each other?" Asami asks, sipping from her cup.

"Our parents used to work together" I explain, "His father and my father were business partners our entire lives."

"Used to?" Mako quizzes, eyebrows raised, "What changed?"

"My father got greedy," Tadashi frowns, "He wanted to use Sakura's healing potions for money. Lei and my father got into a fight and haven't talked since."

I frown, remembering the falling out between my father and his best friend. It was traumatic for everyone. My father and Akio had been friends since their childhood, they did everything together. But one night during our stay in the Fire Nation, things got out of hand and Akio left with Tadashi. I hadn't seen or heard from them since. Until now.

"But you're here now" I smile, "My father would be thrilled"

"Maybe this will be the thing to push our families back together" Tadashi suggests.

Mako sips his drink, eyes carefully watching the young man across from him. My eyes turn back to Tadashi, a smile printed on his lips.

"That would be amazing" I say politely, "It would be just like old times"

"That is so sweet" Asami commented, "Childhood friendships are some of the best"

"I agree" Tadashi charmed, a small smile on his lips.

"Mako and I have always been close, ever since our parents were killed and we were forced to fend for ourselves in the streets as orphans" Bolin said, mouth full of noodles.

An awkward lapse of silence washed over the table, Tadashi taking a moment to absorb the story Bolin had told.

"That is.... terrible" Tadashi frowned, "I'm very sorry to hear that"

Bolin simply shrugged, "We got by, and got away with some cool stories, what do you say, Mako?"

Bolin slapped his older brothers back, Mako's golden eyes moving from the table.

"Oh" he says dumbly, "Yea"

Asami chuckled, reaching for her drink as she watched the older brother stand from the table quickly.

"I have to....um.. do something..."

I press my lips together, watching Mako quickly scurry into his bedroom and sliding the door shut behind him.

Bolin had already moved into another epic story, which captured Tadashi's attention perfectly. My eyes glanced at Asami, who gave me a short, knowing nod.

Clearly, something was wrong.

I got up, moving to the stand outside the door. I knocked, Mako's voice sounding small from the other side.

"Can I come in?" I asked, palm pressed to the door.

"Yea" He replied, allowing me to enter in.

My eyes were met with his slump frame sitting on the bed, his back arched as he balanced his elbows against his knees. His eyes were gloomy, his ora changing from his usual self.

He was upset.

"Is everything okay?" I asked, sitting beside him gently.

"Yeah" He scoffed. "I am responsible for the safety of this famous woman whose family has been kidnapped, while she sits and drinks tea in my living room, all I can think about is how I could fuck up and she could pay the price and-"

"Mako" I stopped him, placing my hand over his. "You're a great police officer, I have felt safe the entire time I've been with you. I trust you"

"I know" He sighed, "I just... this is more pressure then what I'm used to"

"How so?" I asked, mind reeling.

"Because I-" Mako stops himself, "Because you're a famous figure. You're a Shen."

I pause, licking my lips in thought. The air in the room was heavy, drenched in anxiety. I could feel the heat radiate from Mako's hands.

"And you are Mako" I argue back, "You are the man that has fought incredible battles, and stood alongside the Avatar. I can't think of anyone more qualified to be at my side than you"

Mako's lip twitched, the corners of his mouth turning from a frown into a small smile. His shoulders relaxed then, his eyes flashing up to mine.

"And you mean that?"

"I wouldn't lie to you, Mako" I say, eyes never leaving his.

I wanted him to know I meant it. I would never lie to him, ever.

-

Hours later we wave our guests goodbye, Bolin commenting how he could fall asleep on the ground after eating so many bowls of noodles. I give Asami a hug, moving to stand in front of Tadashi.

"Meet me at the police station tomorrow morning" Tadashi says, "My father should be arriving then."

"Alright" I nod, "I look forward to it"

Tadashi smiles, leaning in to place a kiss on my cheek.

"Sleep well, El"

I nod, wishing him goodnight. I turn Asami's lips leaning into my ear.

"Looks like someone is jealous" She whispers, chuckling softly before patting my arm.

I turn around, Mako standing in the doorway with his arms crossed. His eyebrows pushed together as I quickly look away.

"Goodnight!" Bolin sang, bringing up the rear of our line of guests. I wave everyone goodbye, softly closing the door. I turn around:

"Thank you for letting me have everyone-"

I'm cut off by Mako standing directly in front of me. Only a few centimeters away. My breath catches in my throat, stunned by the sudden closeness.

"Who is that guy, Elena?"

"What do you mean?" I look up, his golden eyes already staring back at me. "Tadashi?"

"He's trouble"

"He's an old friend" I correct, moving to step around him.

"An old friend who's father is at odds with your father" Mako corrected, arms folded in front of him. "He disappears when your father and his father get into a fight over money and now he's suddenly back when your family is missing?"

I sigh, moving to sit on the small couch in front of the fireplace.

"I know" I sigh, "I know it looks bad, but he's like family to me. I've known him forever"

"People change Elena," Mako warns, sitting down beside me. "I just want you to be careful around him."

"I will," I say, turning to look at him. "Thank you, for looking out for me"

"It's my job" He smiles, a small chuckle coming from him.

I lean forward to press a kiss to his nose.

"You do it very well"

Chapter 11

The next morning the streets were lined with police carts, officers were standing guard outside the building in large groups. Mako pulls the cart to the curb, turning the engine off before turning to look at me.

"Are you ready?" He asks.

I nod, playing with the hem of my skirt.

I was nervous to see Aiko and I was mortified of what the world would think. The falling out between Aiko and my father was very public, and the second the news broke even more press would come running. The last thing my nerves needed were any more flashing cameras.

"You don't have to do this" Mako stated, voice even and calm. "I can take you home, and make you some tea and you can play piano-"

"I want to go" I say, trying to sound confident. "I want to help"

Mako nods, giving me a firm nod before swinging the driver side door open and running around the front to open mine. There were a few reporters waiting outside, their pen and papers waving in an attempt to grab my attention.

"Elena! Are there any updates on your family?"

"Miss Shen, do you have a comment?"

Mako placed his hand on my side, arm securing around me as he guided me up the front steps and into the building. Once the heavy door closed behind us, I exhaled, running my palms down the front of my skirt.

"That wasn't as bad as I expected," Mako commented, showing his badge to the security officer and leading us through the entrance.

"It will be even worse when Aiko arrives" I state, "It'll be all over the newspapers"

"Then I will buy them all and set them on fire." Mako replied, his voice stern.

I smiled slightly at his ridiculous idea. But part of me was deeply flattered by the offer. Mako had a protective side of him that I simply adored.

We rode up the elevator side by side, the palms of my hands starting the sweat nervously.

"I can feel your heart beating from here" Mako snickered, glancing down at me with his piercing golden eyes.

I look at him wide eyed, a crimson flush running up my cheeks in embarrassment.

"Don't worry" Mako said freely as the elevator bell rang, "Nothing I haven't felt before"

I stare at him, jaw slacked as he smirks and walks away cooly.

Of course he can sense my heart beating so quickly, it beats ten times harder whenever he's around...

I'm quickly shaken from my haze when Tadashi rushes toward me, looping his arm in mine.

"I've been waiting for you, El!"

I smile, letting him lead me through the busy office and into Chief Beifong's office. Men sat around in wooden chairs, a few standing along the walls. I glance around, none of them striking any resemblance. My mind wanders to Mako, curious as to where he had gone off to.

Sat in the leather seat behind the chief's desk was none other than Aiko, my father's old business partner and ex-best friend. He didn't look any different from the last time I saw him. His hair was still a dusty gray. He still dressed his dark clothes and still wore his glasses to the end of his crooked nose.

I wanted to trust him, he was practically family to me- but Mako's words of warning kept echoing in my mind like a siren.

"Elena" He says, standing from his seat, arms spread wide, "Oh my, how you have grown."

My instinct is to walk forward, letting him wrap his arms around me in a welcoming hug. Tadashi stands beside me, a calming smile on his lips.

"Go on, child, have a seat" Aiko says, motioning to the wooden chair on the other side of the desk.

I oblige, turning to glance over my shoulder, in hopes to catch a glimpse of Mako before the wooden door is closed with a click. I turn back, stomach in knots as I watch one of Aiko's entourage pour three cups of tea.

"Jasmine tea is good for the soul" Aiko says, taking the white cup in his hands, "Go on, take a sip"

Tadashi gives me a smile, taking his cup in his hands and bringing it to his lips.

I follow his actions, feeling the steaming drink meet my lips as I take a conservative sip.

"Thank you for coming" I finally say, swallowing the liquid. "My father would appreciate you coming all this way"

"Your father means the world to me" Aiko says, a serious look crossing his features, "A day doesn't go by that I don't regret what happened between your parents and I"

"I know they feel the same," I confess, watching his stern eyes soften.

Perhaps he really does care for my family.

"I came here to offer my services" Aiko says, taking another sip of tea, "It is my understanding that Chief Beifong has appointed the Avatar to lead the search for your family?"

I nod, leaning to set the cup of tea on it's saucer.

Aiko frowns, fingers tapping his chin.

"Well, that will not do" He says sternly, "I have seen the mess that child has caused in this world, I want to hire my own investigators."

"But Korra is the Avatar- she has been trained by the best fighters we have. Not to mention the gifts she has. I don't see anyone better for the job" I defend.

"Then why hasn't she been able to find them?" Aiko points, "I've heard she fought the worst criminals in Republic City, yet she can't locate four defenseless people?"

I close my mouth, pressing my lips shut. Tadashi frowns at me, standing a few steps behind his father. I feel outnumbered, my mind reeling and begging for Mako or Chief Beifong to come in.

"Do you doubt me, child?" Aiko asks, raising an eyebrow.

Before I get a chance to speak, the door bursts open, Chief Beifong stomping in with a stern look on her face. Following close behind are a few officers and Mako, his golden eyes connecting to mine.

"Mr. Nakamura" She spits, "Is there a reason why all the wires to the telephones have been cut?"

I turn, looking wide eyed at Aiko.

"Ah" Aiko smirks, "You must be the famous Chief Beifong" He sayless calmly, leaning back into the leather seat.

"I don't have time for your worthless chatter" She bites, "Explain yourself or you will be escorted out of my station."

Aiko simply chuckles, standing from the chair and turning to gaze out the window.

"That is where you are wrong, Miss Beifong." He says, "I am taking over the investigation now. I didn't see why your station needed any telephones when your officers should be out patrolling the streets. An entire family has been swept away and your officers have been able to do nothing about it. Clearly, they need to spend more time outside, rather than behind a desk. "

"Excuse me?" Beifong says, eyes wide in anger, "I am the chief of this station, and you are not to have any involvement in the Shen case"

"Actually, I do" Aiko smirks, "You see, when Lei Shen moved to Republic City you promised President Raiko you will take good care of them.

Clearly you have failed, which is simply a testament of your ability to run this investigation. Hence, all commanding rights have been given to me"

Aiko tossed a scroll on the table, the freshly inked signature of the President on the bottom stating that the investigation was now led by Aiko Nakamura.

The atmosphere in the room goes cold.

"This is insane" Mako exclaims stepping forward, "You should be a suspect, you and Dr. Shen had a falling out years ago. You can't be trusted."

Aiko simply shrugged, "Every person must learn from his or her mistakes, young man, just like how Miss Beifong will."

With a simple nod, two extremely tall men step forward and grab both of Chief Beifong's arms, holding her still between them.

"That will be all for now" Aiko nods. The men move to escort Beifong out of the room, only to be stopped by a now furious Mako.

I stand, feeling a wave of warmth hit me as Mako stands tall in front of the men, small lips of flames dancing from the palms of his outstretched hands.

"Mako" I gasp.

Aiko laughs, walking calmly toward him.

"Father" Tadashi warns, a worried look on his face.

"It's alright, son," Aiko waves, continuing to walk forward. "Mako will not hurt me, he knows what could happen if he does"

"Mako, please" Beifong sighs, "Stand down. I'll get this sorted with President Raiko"

Mako nods, closing his palms and extinguishing the flames. He relaxes a bit, stepping aside to let the men take Beifong away.

"Elena, let's go." he says, turning to me.

I open my mouth, only for Aiko to wrap an arm around my shoulders.

"She is too busy now, child." Aiko says, "We must begin our work to bring her family home"

"Elena" Mako says again. Golden eyes staring at me unwavering.

I could feel the nerves pulsing in my veins. The last thing I wanted was a showdown between Mako and Aiko. Spirits knew how that would end.

"Aiko" I said with a shaking breath, "I am going to go with Mako, just to make sure everything is alright"

Aiko frowned, "We must not waste any time"

"I won't be long" I rushed, "I promise"

Without allowing him to say another word, I walk forward. Mako turns to lead us out of the office and into the now empty desks of the police station.

Mako presses the button to call the elevator, his right hand reaching out to grab mine. I could feel the heat radiating from his palms. He was pulsing with anger. I gulp, looking over my shoulder to see Aiko's men closing the double doors to Chief Beifong's office.

"Mako" I say, feeling the palm against mine get warmer each passing second. "Mako"

The bell rings and the doors open, Mako quickly stepping in and pulling me with him. He pushes the button to the ground floor and exhales, letting go of my hand to rub his palms against his face.

"I don't know what happened in there" He says, muffed by his hands. "Why would President Raiko give all the commanding power to Aiko? This doesn't make any sense"

"Then let's go visit Raiko" I say, "I'm sure he'll see me if I go"

"This doesn't feel right" Mako sighs, "None of this does"

"Aiko has a way of taking over things" I sigh, leaning against the wall of the elevator. "I remember him and my father getting into arguments because Aiko likes to be in command of things"

"It's not just that.." Mako says quietly, watching the doors open with a ding.

We walk outside and are once again circled by cameras, bright white lights flashing from every direction as I move swiftly toward Mako's cart.

"Elena!" a report yelled, "Any word on your family?"

"No" I reply, turning to face the man with the giant camera, "We are still trying"

"Anything you'd like to say to them?"

I gulp, seeing Mako watching me in the corner of my eye.

"I love them" I say, a wave of sadness washing over me. "And that I will find them soon. We won't rest until they are home safe"

More reporters begin to yell questions, the flashing of cameras overwhelming. Mako grabs my hand and escorts me the rest of the way to his cart, opening my side's door. I sit with a sigh, tilting my head back against the cushioned seat as he gets in.

"You really shouldn't talk to them" Mako points, "They will always twist your words"

I shrug, looking at the crowd while he starts the cart.

"I just want my family to know I'm trying"

"Of course they know that," Mako says, pulling out onto the road. "What makes you think they wouldn't?"

I shrug again, looking down at my fingers.

"I don't know" I say, "I guess I have never been the type of person to be the hero. I'm usually just a side character."

"What do you mean?" He asks, glancing over at me.

"I see myself as a supporting actor in a mover." I say, "I'm not a Nuktuk"

"No one is a Nuktuk..." Mako says freely. "Nuktuk isn't a real person"

"I know that" I roll my eyes. "I'm just saying I have never been the person to run towards all the action. I'm usually the girl who is in the crowd cheering when the battle is won by the hero at the end of the mover."

"Then be the hero" Mako says.

"It's not that easy" I point out, looking outside at the passing streets, "Heroes are brave and fearless. I'm scared of everything."

Mako chuckles, "I doubt you are afraid of everything, El"

"No, really" I giggle, "I am scared of bugs, have you ever seen a Giant Fly? Terrifying"

Mako rolls his eyes, "Everyone is afraid of Giant Flies" He points out with a chuckle. Then says seriously: "You can be the hero, all you have to do is believe in yourself. You have faced this entire situation bravely."

"Because I have to be brave" I argue. "My family is on the lie"

"Exactly" Mako says, "This is scary. But you are brave. You are going to be the hero in this story, Elena. I know it."

A small smile spreads on my lips. It felt good to hear him say that.

Mako believes in me.

Maybe I can be the hero...

Chapter 12

Mako-

The president's residence was huge. It was a stone building that sat in the middle of a sprawling green yard. Flowers were sprinkled around the front as guards were posted at every entrance of the property.

I stood with my hands in my pockets as Elena talked to one of the guards, her face showing a sad expression as the guard shook his head. Her shoulders slumped in obvious defeat.

I could feel the warmth in my body grow in anger as she turned and walked toward me, a frown gracing her beautiful face.

"They won't let me see the president," She said, stopping a few steps in front of me.

"Why?" I quipped, my patience quickly running thin. "This is nonsense. First the Chief and now the president won't see you?"

Elena shrugs, opening her mouth to say something only to close it a moment later. It was clear she was at a loss for words.

I huff, hands on my hips as I look at the guards.

"Let me try talking to them" I announce, taking a step forward.

"Mako" Elena warned, "Please be careful"

I know she doesnt mean for me to actually be careful. She wants me to watch my temper. We both knew I could have a short fuse... literally.

"Hey" I say, my voice firm. "Officer Mako, I'm with the Republic City Police"

"Sorry kid" the guard says, one hand lazily sitting in his pocket. "I got strict orders to not let anyone in"

"This is regarding the Shen case" I say, "That's Elena Shen"

The man follows my outstretched finger, his eyes landing on Elena who stood nervously nearby. He shrugs, in disinterest.

"Orders are orders, kid"

That's it.

I feel the temperature in my palms spike as the blood begins to pump in my veins.

"You have no idea who you are talking to," I growl. "That is Elena Shen and she needs to talk to the president now. With or without your permission."

A small hand wraps around my upper arm, causing me to turn away from the now terrified guard.

"Mako" Elena says softly, eyes wide. "Let's go. We can try something else"

I sigh, balling my fingers into a tight fist.

"Fine" I grumble, turning away sharply to walk back to my police kart.

I get in and slam the door, hands gripping the steering wheel tightly.

"There has to be a way inside" Elena says, shutting the door.

"This is all bullshit" I say, "Something is going on. Aiko did something"

"We don't know that" Elena points, turning to look at me. "This is probably a huge misunderstanding"

I huff, turning the ignition and pulling out onto the road.

Silence wraps around us as we drive. I know I lost my temper back there, but what was I supposed to do?

Aiko is clearly the one behind this. Why would Raiko sign over all the commanding rights to Aiko? Why won't the president see Elena?

I pull up in front of my building and park, turning the kart off and turn to Elena.

"I'm sorry if I freaked you out" I say, reaching up to mindlessly rub the back of my neck. "I didn't mean to"

Elena smiles gently, her perfectly lined teeth a bright white.

"I know don't you mean to" she says kindly, "We are on the same team, we share the same frustrations"

"I just feel like we lost control of this case" I sigh, "All of our resources...g one- just like that"

"We'll figure this out," She says. "But we won't accomplish anything sitting in here"

She turns to open the door and I follow, closing my own before going inside my tiny apartment.

What a day.

-Elena-

I didn't realize how tight my muscles were until I took a long shower. The water was like therapy against my skin. I stood under the falling drops for a long time, letting it wash away stress from the day.

My mind kept replaying the day's events.

Aiko was back. Chief Beifong was gone.

It all felt like too much. My mind was constantly reeling with information. I was trying my best to process it all, but it was growing to be too much to handle.

I sigh, turning the switch of the water. I carefully step out, pulling the curtain open.

A cough makes me look up in surprise, a pair of golden eyes staring back at me in the mirror of the bathroom.

"Oh my-" I say, quickly using the curtain of the shower to cover my body.

"I'm sorry, I was just-" Mako mumbles, quickly turning away.

"It's okay" I say, a blush crawling up my cheeks.

He closes the door with a thud, leaving my heart pulsing in my chest.

A few minutes later I step out, a white dress on as I tie my hair back in a neat braid. The smell of noodles floats around the room, making my stomach growl in hunger.

I step into the main room, Mako's back turned to me as he cooked.

"It smells good" I say, trying to act normal.

He literally just saw me naked.

"Thanks" He says, not turning to look at me.

Great. Now we are awkward.

I sit on the seat of my small piano, looking at my nails.

A few more minutes pass and then a knock sounds from the front door.

I jump up, relieved.

"I'll get it!"

I open the door to see Bolin standing on the other side, Pabu sitting cutely on his shoulder.

"Evening friends!" Bolin greets, stepping inside. "It smells great in here"

"Mako is making noodles" I say, closing the door behind him.

"We came at the right time, Pabu" Bolin grins, helping the furry ferret down from his shoulder.

Bolin leans against the counter, an inquisitive look in his eye.

"I saw the papers today" he begins, "Beifong was taken off command?"

"Yeah" Mako scoffs, moving to add a few spices into the boiling pot, "Elena and I went to the president's office to try and talk to him and he refused to see us. Dr. Shen's old business partner Aiko was apparently appointed to be the new commander of the search"

"Isn't that the guy that your father got into a fight with?" Bolin asks, turning to look at me.

"It happened a while ago" I say, "But yes, it is."

Bolin chuckles, "He's totally guilty"

Mako looks over his shoulder at me, as if to say 'I told you so'

"We don't know that for sure" I defend.

"Oh come on" Bolin whines, "This is a textbook villain. Old friend turned foe is out to get your family and is now sabotaging the search for them. I just read a script at the studio with this exact story line."

"This isn't a mover, Bolin" I frown, "And sure, we should be careful, but we can't assume the worst until we have more evidence."

"I think he is suspect number 1" Bolin says, hands up in defense, "Mako, do you agree?"

"You bet" Mako says, turning off the stove top. "But we have to be smart. If Aiko really is guilty, we need to stick around and see if he gives us any clues."

"Like a spy!" Bolin grins

Mako rolls his eyes.

"Then I'll go back to the station tomorrow and see what I can find out" I say, watching as Mako hands bowls of noodles to Bolin and I. "Either him or Tadashi will give me something to work with"

"Elena the spy" Bolin says, hands in the air excited. "What a great title for a mover"

"Bolin" Mako groans, "Enough with the movers, please"

"Mako, my friend" Bolin says, setting a hand on his brother's shoulder. "Movers are the future."

"When do we get to sacrifice Bolin in this plan?" Mako asks, a chuckle escaping his lips.

I grin, picking up my chopsticks.

Sure, this was stressful. But at least I got to cherish these good moments.

Chapter 13

A group of servers lined the blood red walls of the private dining room. Each of them wore the same perfectly ironed black uniform. A few of them held pitchers of drinks, and a few held trays of various food items.

During my upbringing, my parents had been invited to many fancy restaurants. Throughout the years my family and I had become used to the ultra-elite dining places around the different cities.

But nothing was like Koda's.

Koda's was a high end steak restaurant that Asami frequented. Ever since she took over her father's business, the establishment had become a key part of her business handlings.

"Try some of the sauce" She smiled, motioning for me to try a small rose red liquid in a small cup on the table "It has ginger in it- it is amazing"

I pick up a small slice of steak and dip it in the sauce and bring it to my mouth to taste.

Like always, Asami was right. It was delicious.

"Do you like it?" She asks, a small smile on her lips.

"It's incredible" I reply, gently sitting my chopsticks on the plate in front of me.

It had been a week since Aiko arrived in Republic City. I had been keeping myself busy in meetings with Aiko and his affiliates. Aiko had been able to contact some of his business partners around the world and even hire a few private investigators to join the case.

All of it sounded nice- but in reality we hadn't made any progress.

Mako was kept busy with the station. Ever since Beifong was demoted, all the officers were told to patrol the streets. Mako had been coming home in the middle of the night since then, exhausted. I even caught him asleep on the couch still in his uniform one night.

Tonight, Asami had invited me out to a nice dinner, in hopes to lighten my mood. It was a very kind gesture, but it wasn't really working.

"Are you alright?" Asami says, noticing my disconnected gaze.

I blink, inhaling quickly as I snap back to reality.

"Yea" I say, "I'm sorry. I just have a lot going through my mind"

Asami nods knowingly, "You don't have to apologize. I invited you here to hang out, but I also wanted you to know that I am here to help."

I look up at her in surprise. Her expression was sincere.

"Future Industries has a lot of contacts around the world. Including a lot outside of Republic City. I was thinking I could reach out to a few to see if they could help us"

I look at her in surprise. Her kindness always blew me away.

"But you're so busy" I say, "I could never ask that of you"

"You are a part of this team now, Elena" Asami smiles, "That is what we do for each other."

I smile, feeling tears well up in my eyes.

It was overwhelmingly kind of her to say that. Ever since my family was taken I had felt so out of place. It was nice to feel like I belonged somewhere.

"Thank you" I say, "Truly"

Asami smiles, reaching forward to sip from her glass when the door to our dining room slides open. We turn, a finely dressed looking Tadashi in the doorway.

"I thought I heard your voice" He grins, walking forward. He turns and gives Asami a small bow, "It is lovely to see you again, Miss Sato"

Asami nods politely, sipping her drink again. Tadashi turns to me, sighing.

"I have been meaning to talk to you, El" He says, "I am so sorry for how my father handled Chief Beifong. You know how he can be sometimes"

I nod giving him a polite smile, "Thank you for saying that. It was a lot to take in."

Tadashi nods, "Understandable. I can imagine how confusing it must have been to receive the news so suddenly. With President Raiko being in Ba Sing Se, I'm sure it was hard to hear the news from my father"

I nod again, watching Tadashi look between Asami and I.

A beat of silence surrounds us.

"Well" Tadashi says, clasping his hands together, "I must be going. I hope you ladies enjoy your dinner. Elena, I will see you tomorrow."

He bows once more and then exits, the door sliding back in his place.

Asami stands up abruptly, tossing the napkin on her plate as she steps away from the table.

"Where are you going?" I ask, pushing my chair away from the table.

"To follow him" Asami says, "Raiko isn't in Ba Sing Se, he never was."

"How do you know?" I ask, watching her slide the dining room door open.

"I had a meeting with him and a few of my executive board members. His office canceled because they said he wasn't feeling well" Asami says. "Something is wrong. Very wrong."

-Mako-

I close the front door lazily, tossing my coat on the hanger as I slide off my shoes. I was exhausted. From sunup to sundown, we have been walking the streets. I missed being in the action. All I had been dealing with is parking tickets and helping old ladies cross the busy street. It was torture.

I sit on my couch and tilt my head back, exhaling.

"Elena" I call, keeping my eyes closed.

Nothing.

I frown, tilting my head back up and opening my eyes. "Elena, are you here?"

Nothing again.

I groan, standing up from my seat and peek into my bedroom and washroom. Both empty.

"Where did she go?"

The phone begins to ring, the chime echoing around my apartment. I walk over, picking up the receiver and holding it to my ear.

"Hello?"

"Mako, it's me," Elena says on the other line. "How fast can you get to Asami's office?"

"What?" I ask, "Why?"

"We caught Tadashi in a lie" She says on the other line. "Asami and I are going to go to the President's palace to check it out"

I quickly use my shoulder to hold the phone to my ear, moving to grab my shoes.

"That sounds dangerous" I say, "Wait for me."

"We don't have much time!" Asami says in the background. "Spirits know what could be going on"

"Does Bolin know?" I ask, "We could use his help"

"I'll call him" Elena says, "Get here quick"

"Alright"

I slam the phone back on its holder and quickly slide my shoes on.

I make it to Asami's office downtown within minutes, thanks to the blinking siren lights on my police kart.

The office entry is empty, a light on in the back office letting me know where to go. The room is large, wall to wall windows showing a breathtaking view of the city.

Asami's office was some of the best real estate in the world.

"You made it" Asami smiles.

She was dressed in a deep red dress, her hair pinned up in a neat bun. Beside her sat Elena, her legs dangled beneath her as she sat on Asami's desk. Her dress was light blue, the sleeves just cupping her upper arms. Her hair was curled and thrown over her shoulder carelessly.

She looked beautiful.

Bolin had somehow arrived before I did. He stood in the back, looking over a notebook on Asami's desk.

"What happened?" I ask, look between the two women.

"We saw Tadashi at dinner and caught him up in a lie" Elena says, a frown on her lips. "He said President Raiko was out of town, but Asami and her company had an appointment with him but it was canceled because they told her he was sick."

I frown, wrapping my arms in front of my chest.

"So, what do we do now? We know they are lying. Are we going to confront them?" I ask.

"Not yet" Asami says, "We need more evidence"

"We have evidence" I correct, "You said you caught Tadashi in a lie, that is enough to take to Chief Beifong"

"No, there is more going on" Asami says, "We have a feeling"

"Asami is picking up Korra's avatar senses," Bolin jokes, walking to stand beside me.

"So what do we do?" I ask, ignoring my brother's childish comments.

"We use this," Asami says, holding a small metal oval in the palm of her hand.

It was tiny, just smaller than her palm.

"What are we looking at?" Bolin asks dumbly, staring at the object in confusion.

"This is the Spy Bug 1000, a new design by Future Industries" Asami grins proudly, using her finger to click a small button.

The oval then grows mechanical legs and antennas, the once useless scrap of metal taking the form of a small beetle.

"It's a prototype, but I think it will do the job well," Asami says, placing the small machine on her desk. "It's controlled by this remote with a speaker. The microphone on the Bug will feed into the speaker and allow us to hear anything in real time"

Asami picks up the black remote and holds it in her hands, clicking a button. The bug jumps to life, crawling around her desk. It looked so lifelike. To the naked eye, you wouldn't expect it to be a robot.

"That is brilliant" Elena says, bending down to see it closer. "So we will take this to the president's mansion to see what's really going on?"

"Exactly" Asami nods, moving the small button around to make the robot move.

"It's kinda creepy" Bolin winces, watching the bug hop around.

"It's accurate to the size and shape of a real beetle, which is why it is the perfect spy device. If hidden well, no one will suspect a thing" Asami says proudly.

"Well, what are we waiting for?" I say, "Get the creepy robot bug and let's go."

Chapter 14

The air was crisp as we got out of Mako's kart. My arms crossed over my chest in an attempt to hold warmth. We parked a few blocks away from the President's property and walked closer. Mako's shoulder brushing against mine as we walked.

"How are you?" He asked, looking down at me.

"Good" I reply, "Hopeful. I really want this to give us some clues"

Mako nods understandingly.

"Asami is smart, I think this will give us something to work with"

I nod in agreement, watching Bolin and Asami walk a few steps in front of us. It had been a few days since Mako and I got to talk by ourselves. Part of me had been longing to be alone with him again.

He clears his throat, causing me to glance over at him.

"You- uh" He stutters, "You look beautiful tonight"

A blush crawls up my cheeks, causing me to bashfully look down.

"Thanks" I say, looking back at him after a moment. "You look handsome too"

He gives me a small smile, his golden eyes looking at me softly.

He was breathtakingly handsome. The silver moonlight mixed with the amber street lights made him look like a priceless piece of art.

My entire life I had been wondering what it would be like to feel this way for someone. To look at them and feel this heavenly warm feeling. I saw it between my parents, and I saw it briefly between Vera and Iroh. It was a beautiful thing to see between two people. The immense amount of care and consideration, mixed with adoration - and for the first time in my life I was starting to feel that way too. For Mako.

"You lovebirds still back there?"

I look up in surprise, Bolin giggling in front of us.

Mako rolls his eyes, muttering a soft 'Sorry about him' under his breath.

"This is the spot." Asmai says. Looking up a large stone wall that held the backside of the President's home. "There should be a vent along this wall, that is where we can put the bug in to get it inside"

"What happens if it gets squashed?" Bolin asks, hands on his hips.

A beat of silence.

"Let's try not to think about that... " Asami says, bending down to take the small capsule out of her pocket. With a click it morphs into its true form, the robotic bug crawling to life.

As much as I hated to admit it, Bolin was right. It was creepy.

Asami takes out the controller and the bug jumps down, crawling on the ground and into the small vent on the wall.

"We are in" Asami says happily, "All we need to do now is station the bug in a good spot and listen"

"Sounds easy enough" Mako comments.

"Hey!" We turn, a guard walking toward us quickly with two more following close behind. "What are you doing back there?"

Asami quickly shoves the control in her dress pocket.

"We were just on a walk" I say innocently, the guard stopping a few steps ahead of us.

"At this time of night?" one asks, his eyebrow raised in question.

"My brother is allergic to sunlight," Bolin says confidently, making us all glance at him. "He can only go outside at night or else he'll break into some really nasty hives. It's not pretty."

The guards exchange bewildered looks between each other.

"We'll get going now" Asami says, not allowing the guards to respond. "Have a lovely evening!"

Asami grabs my arm quickly and walks us past the guards, our steps fast.

"Allergic to the sun?" Mako hisses at Bolin, "What does that even mean?"

"It could be possible! I'm not a doctor." Bolin shrugs, hands up in defense.

Mako rolls his eyes and unlocks the kart, each of us getting in. I slide in the passenger seat beside Mako, closing the door tightly.

"What a rush!" I say, grinning. My blood is pumping quickly in my veins with adrenaline. "That was such a thrill!"

Asami chuckles, leaning up the front of the kart, "I'm assuming that's the first time you have ever broken into a building?"

"Yea, but it was so fun!" I exclaim. "Breaking and entering wasn't exactly a Shen family activity"

Everyone laughs, Mako starting the engine and pulling onto the road.

"Well, we are happy your first crime was spent with us" Bolin says, a hand over his heart to show sincerity. "It's an honor, Miss Shen"

"Alright, so what's the plan now?" Mako says, pulling the group back to focus.

"Bolin and I will come back tomorrow to get the bug in a good position" Asami says, "Elena, try to find out more information tomorrow at the station."

"I don't think she should go back to the station" Mako says, knuckles gripping the steering wheel tightly. "We know Tadashi and Aiko are up to no good. It could be dangerous"

I frown, turning my head to look at him, "But I have to go back, they will suspect something is wrong if I don't."

Mako sighs heavily, a frown present on his lips.

"I don't like it." He states.

"Elena is right" Asami says, "We have to gather more information. Having Elena by Aiko's side could be really useful"

"But it could also be deadly." Mako snaps.

Asami presses her lips together and leans back, eyes tamed out the window.

"I'll be okay" I say, reaching over to place my palm on Mako's shoulder. "I promise"

-Mako

The next morning was cold, the wind dancing off the water and engulfing me in a chill. I can't imagine what it would be like to be a non-firebender during the cold months. I would turn into a living ice cube.

I lean against my kart, arms folded in front of me as I watch an old man illegally park his vehicle across the street. He was carrying two large baskets of fruit, each overflowing with citrus. I watch him silently, not motivated to write him a ticket.

My mind kept going back to last night. After we dropped off Asami and Bolin, Elena and I silently finished our drive back to my apartment. I knew I was being too controlling, but the mere thought of something happening to her made my head spin. I physically could not handle it.

"I'm sorry I snapped at you" I said, watching her slip off her shoes in my doorway.

She looked up at me with a small smile, "It's okay. I know you are just being protective. But I have to do this Mako, you know that."

"I know" I sighed, running a hand over my face, "and I know we've had this conversation before. I just can't stand you being around those guys. They are trouble."

She walked up to me then. Her small hand reached up to cup my cheek. Her skin was soft like silk. It was the most comforting gesture I had ever received. Her eyes looked up into mine, those breathtaking blue irises pulling me in like a spell.

I leaned my head down, forehead resting gently against hers. I could feel her breath against my face, her chest rising and falling quickly with excitement. She knew I wanted to kiss her, and I knew I was going to.

So I did.

I closed the small gap and kissed her, both of my hands reaching up to wrap around her small waist. I felt her arms wrap around my neck, pulling me closer to her. We stood there wrapped in each other's embrace for a few minutes. Her lips danced against mine.

I was starting to feel flushed, my adrenaline kicking into overdrive. The physical effects she had on me were clear- and frankly painful in my trousers.

I stepped back, slyly reaching down to pull the hem of my tunic down in hopes to conceal my... predicament. Luckily for me, she didn't seem to notice.

"Goodnight, Mako" She purred, her arms falling back to her sides as she stepped back.

I stood there dumbly in the middle of my apartment, just like I was now in the middle of the street.

The static of my kart radio broke me from my thoughts, making me jump into action and lean over the driver side.

"This is Mako" I said, holding the microphone in my hand.

"All units report to the station" the voice said, "Avatar Korra has returned."

Chapter 15

I sat with my legs crossed, my eyes tamed on the ticking clock that hung on the back wall. The wooden chair I sat in was starting to make my backache, the stiff wooden planks giving my body no comfortable support.

Aiko sat at Chief Beifong's desk, his arms folded in front of him as one of his henchmen went over the list of updates from his colleagues around the world. I zoned out after the first one, already well aware that we had made no progress.

A man opened the door, his eyes wide in excitement. He was panting, his chest rising and falling as if he had just finished a marathon.

"She has returned" He exhaled, "Avatar Korra has returned to Republic City"

I stood in surprise, my arms falling dumbly to my sides.

"Wait here" Aiko demands, his eyebrows pushed together.

The man steps aside, allowing Aiko to exit the office. Tadashi is a few steps behind his father, just passing the first few desks of the station when the door bursts open.

I stand in the doorway, watching a tall tanned woman walk through the swinging doors. She wore all blue, her brown hair tied back with ribbon. Her muscles were toned and prominent. It was clear she was Avatar Korra.

"What is the meaning of this?" Aiko snaps, walking up to the young woman.

"I would stop right there" She growls, "I won't hesitate"

Aiko chuckles, nodding his head in mocking approval.

"I wouldn't expect any less of you, Miss Avatar" he hisses, "You are always one to make a mess"

"Where is Lin Beifong?" Korra asks, ignoring Aiko's taunts.

"She was demoted." Aiko replies monotonically, "She was no use to this department"

"That is bullshit" Korra snaps, "How could this happen?"

"Watch your tongue, girl" Aiko says, his tone dark, "The President himself signed it into action"

Korra's eyes are beaming with anger, her arms rising from her sides as a swirl of wind blows around the room. The force makes papers fly, books soaring off the shelves. Aiko is knocked back onto his butt, along with the small group of henchmen around him.

I am shoved back against the wall with a thud, my back and tailbone sharp with pain.

"Korra!"

I look up, slowly getting back to my feet. Mako walks in, followed by a few officers. He rushes to her, eyes wide in shock at the chaotic scene around him.

"This girl needs to be controlled" Aiko hisses, rising back to his feet. "Please escort her out of this building. She belongs on Air Temple Island, away from civilization"

"What is going on?" Korra asks, turning to Mako.

"It's a lot to explain" Mako sighs, "Let's go"

"Who is that douchebag?" Korra says, ignoring Mako's request.

"I am the leader of this search," Aiko says, "Which you have interrupted."

"Did Raiko really put him in charge?" Korra asks, a look of disbelief on her face.

"I'll explain later" Mako repeats, "Let's go"

He gently grabs her upper arm, as if demanding her to follow him. He looks over at me, nudging his head forward to tell me to follow along.

I nod, quickly walking behind them as Aiko instructs his men to clean the now disheveled station.

"Are you alright?" Mako asks, a small hand placed on my lower back.

"I'm fine" I smile gently, "It's not everyday you get knocked over by the Avatar"

"You must be Elena Shen" Korra says, hand outstretched. "I'm Korra"

"It's an honor" I say, shaking her hand. "Thank you for helping us find my family"

"It's nothing" Korra says, waving her hand nonchalantly. "It's just what Avatars do"

"It's time we catch you up" Mako says, "Let's go to my place"

-Mako-

Clouds of steam climb toward the ceiling of my living room. Bowls of hot noodles sit in front of each of us. If it weren't for the task at hand, I would be overjoyed. This is the first meal we have shared together in a long time.

"So you bugged the President's mansion?" Korra asks, using her set of chopsticks to stir the bowl in front of her.

"You bet"Asami says, sitting beside her.

"That is genius" Korra compliments, "We will definitely catch them in a lie"

"I hope so," Elena chimes, dabbing her mouth with a napkin. "I don't know how much longer we have"

"Sure" Korra nods in understanding, looking down at the table. "In these cases, we usually have a matter of weeks. Because of your family's status in society, we may have more time."

"Do you think their abductors will want ransom?" I ask, looking at her.

"It's possible." Korra says.

"I have access to our family account at the Republic City Bank" Elena adds, looking at Korra.

"No" Korra replies, "We won't pay the ransom. If we get any offers from their abductors, we would just trace it back to their location and rescue them without paying."

"Oh" Elena says, a frown on her lips.

"Don't worry, El" Asami smiles, reaching over to pat her shoulder, "We are making more progress everyday. We will bring them home soon"

I notice Elena's eyes begin to water. Her chin pointed down at her lap.

"Do you want some desert?" I ask her, trying to break her from her anxious thoughts. "I have that melon ice cream you love"

She looks up, blue eyes still sparkling with sadness. A small smile spreads on her lips, leading her to give me a nod in approval.

I stand, rushing over to prepare her desert. As I am scooping up some of the frozen treat, I feel Korra stand beside me, her shoulder brushing mine.

"I've been looking forward to seeing you" She says quietly.

I turn to her in shock, not expecting her comment. Her tone was low and almost sensual.

"Korra..." I begin, a frown on my lips.

"I know things were rough between us" She interrupts. "But being away from the city made me think and... I don't know.... Maybe miss you and us?"

I listen to her in surprise, her mood shifting from flirty to sad.

"I thought about you a lot, Mako"

"Korra, please" I say, overwhelmed. "I don't think that is a good idea"

Her icy blue eyes look up at me in distress, like she had just heard heartbreaking news.

"Why?" She asks.

My fingers fumble with the scoop and drop it into the bowl with a clang. I sigh in frustration picking it up to try and scoop another mound of ice cream.

"I have moved on" I confess, "And you should too"

I can feel her absorb my words. I glance to look at her. She swallows hard, giving me a soft nod. She was upset.

"Who is she?" She asks, pleading.

"Korra, I am not going to tell you that" I say seriously.

She rolls her eyes angrily. "Why not?"

"Because!" I say, closing the top of the ice cream container. "Because, I don't think it's necessary."

"Mako" Korra says, taking hold of my hand. "I am going to win you back."

I press my lips together. There was no point in fighting over it, her classic stubbornness would block out anything I try to say.

So I stay silent, taking the ice cream and putting it back in the icebox.

"Here's your bowl" I say, handing her a red ceramic bowl full of ice cream before walking away.

"So she just... told you that? In the middle of your kitchen?"

"Yeah" I say, setting my water bottle down on the floor. "It was so awkward."

Bolin and I are in the gym, doing our weekly joint workout. When he was cast in a mover that scripted him with 'dazzling washboard abs', he enlisted me to be his trainer. So, once a week we go to the gym connected to the police headquarters.

"I can imagine" He says, lying on the bench to prepare to lift some weights. "Does Elena know?"

"No" I say, shaking my head.

I watch Bolin in the mirror, the heavy metal weights being lifted above his head a few times before he sets it back on the stand and sits up.

"This is going to cause a lot of problems" He says, wiping the sweat from his brow.

"How so?" I ask, picking up a small hand-held weight.

"You are constantly with 3 women who you have either been romantically involved with or are currently involved with. How could that not be trouble?"

"Asami and Elena get along great" I argue, lifting the weight in my hands. "And Korra will get along too, she just needs to get over me."

Bolin chuckles, "Whatever you say, big bro"

I roll my eyes, counting each time I lift the weight before switching it to my other hand. Bolin does a few more exercises before he switches to a treadmill.

"So are you and Elena, like, dating?" He asks.

I shrug, "I guess we haven't specified what we are. She has a lot to worry about, the last thing she needs is something else on her plate"

"She might like having the label" Bolin suggests, "Girls are weird like that"

"Do you think it will make her feel better? Like, help her take her mind off things?" I ask.

Bolin shrugs, "Probably. Girls love bragging about their boyfriends. I'm sure it will be a welcomed distraction"

I nod, reaching to wipe the sweat from my face with my shirt.

"Bolin, that might be the most helpful thing you have ever told me"

A/N: Hi everyone! First, thank you for all the reads! I saw today we are Number 2 in the LegendOfKorra tag! THANK YOU!!

I wanted to update you all on a few things:

1) I will now be updating this story every Wednesday going forward. There may be additional updates (if my personal schedule allows), but you will always seen an update on Wednesdays weekly.

2) I have updated the rating of this story to be MATURE. I am currently writing the next chapter and it will include some sexual themes and conversations (spoiler!!!). All characters in the book that would partake in sexual activities are 18+.

3) I see I have readers from all over the world, which is SO COOL! So far this story has reached North & South America, Europe, and Asia. I love to travel, so seeing my work being read all over the globe is such an amazing feeling. If you want, please comment your favorite place to visit in your home country. I am looking for a place to vacation this summer, so I need your ideas!

Chapter 16

It feels like years since I sat at the bench. My fingers sliding over the pearl white keys before pressing them down to strike a bold chord. I move my fingers up and down the row, an unknown melody coming to life around me. I sway my head to the beat, improvising my movements.

It felt good to be playing again. I could feel the stress in my body flow through my arms and into the piano. This had been a perfect form of therapy for me ever since I touched a piano.

Korra had returned yesterday, and today we were thrusted into more commotion. Asami had been spending her days using the robotic bug to sneak about the President's Mansion, in hopes to overhear a clue. So far the efforts had been fruitless, but she was remaining hopeful.

The door to the tiny apartment opens, Mako giving me a small smile before closing it behind him. He slides off his shoes, untying his scarf and undoing his coat to hang them neatly on the hanger.

I lift my hands, the music fading to silence.

"How are you?" I ask.

"Tired," Mako says, "But I ran into Asami outside. She says she heard something that could be useful"

I perk up, standing from my seat. "What is it?"

"Aiko is going to visit the mansion tomorrow at lunchtime" Mako says, "He is meeting with the President."

"That is great!" I exclaim, "We are bound to hear something then!"

"I think so too" Mako says.

I gleefully jump into his arms, wrapping him up in a tight hug. He does the same, wrapping his arms around my waist and pulling me close. We stand there for a few moments, enjoying each other's presence.

I lean away, my arms still wrapped around his neck and resting on his shoulders.

"Thank you, Mako" I say softly, "For everything"

"You say that a lot" Mako says, reaching up to trace my cheek with his pointer finger softly.

"I was raised to have good manners" I joke, "Can't exactly be rude to the Fire Lord"

Mako chuckles, his eyes squinting as he shows his brilliant smile. I take a moment to admire how handsome he looked when he laughed.

"I've been thinking..." He begins, golden eyes looking deep into mine. "There has been something I have been wanting to ask you"

"What is it?" I ask, eyebrow raised.

"Do you want to be my girlfriend?"

I gasp in surprise, a sense of excitement flowing over me. I had never had anyone ask me that before.

"Yes" I grin, "Yes!"

He smiles back, leaning in to give me a kiss.

I melt into him, my body relaxing into the embrace. My mind is reeling. I have a boyfriend!

He pulls away exhaling, his breath fanning over my face.

"Don't stop" I say softly, looking at him with hooded eyes. "Please"

"Always so polite" Mako muses, nudging his nose with mine.

I lean and kiss him again, this time harder and more hungry. He reacts, pulling me against him so our bodies are completely touching.

I feel our lips dance together, each of us taking time to explore the other. The heat begins to rise around me, both from attraction and the heat radiating off of Mako.

I feel his hands snake around my body, one on my cheek to hold me in place and the other exploring my back. My palms are on his chest, fingers clinging to the fabric of his shirt. I felt if I let go, I may fall over.

After a few more minutes I feel him step forward, my legs reacting and following his other footsteps until I feel the arm of the couch behind me. I break away, panting as I look at him through a haze.

"You are so gorgeous" He exhales, reaching forward to brush a strand of hair from my face. "Stunning."

A blush illuminates my cheeks, causing me to meekly look away.

"Hey" He says, using his fingers to make me turn back to him, "Don't be embarrassed. You are truly the most beautiful woman I have ever seen"

I open my mouth to protest, but his lips connect to mind and my words are lost.

I'm leaning against the side of the couch, Mako leaning over me as our embrace continues.

His hands continue their adventure around my body, his warm palms finding themselves nestled on my hips under my shirt. The warmth radiating off him is intoxicating, a shiver rolling through me.

I feel him slowly inch his hands up, toward my chest. I sense his hesitation, breaking our embrace to smile at him softly.

"Touch me, Mako" I say, my chest having, "It's okay"

He groans in approval, sliding both his hands all the way up my chest and resting on my breasts. I am absolutely melting. The sensations coming over me are something I had never felt before. It was exciting and intoxicatingly addicting.

His palms move over my breasts, his fingers squeezing them gently. I involuntarily moan in response. It felt like a bolt of electricity had shot through me.

He pulls away from my face, his pulp lips tracing delicate kisses down my cheek, chin, and then finally my neck. My fingers fan into his hair, tugging at the strands lightly in response.

He stops, coming back to face me and giving me one last chase peck on the lips. His chest is heaving and cheeks flushed. His golden eyes could barely be seen over the blackness of his pupils.

"Can I ask you something?" He says in a husky voice, reaching down to take my hands in his.

"Anything" I reply sincerely. I'd tell him anything he wanted to know.

"Have you ever.." He clears his throat nervously, "Have you ever had sex?"

I open my mouth in shock, my cheeks dancing with redness.

"No" I say honestly, "I haven't. Have you?"

He nods, squeezing my hands adoringly, "I don't want you to feel rushed. It's a big deal, and I want you to make the right decision. I won't pressure you"

"I know" I say, "I trust you."

"I'll take care of you when the time comes" He smiles, "We will work up to it, so you feel comfortable."

"Thank you" I smile, wrapping him up in a tight hug.

Mako, my boyfriend. I like the sound of that.

-Mako -

I didn't experience a lot of feelings of peace growing up. Past the age of 8, I never thought of sleep as a form of relaxation- only as a way to refuel my body so I can live to see another day.

Today, however, I can't help but think that this was what I was missing all those years. There she is, peacefully asleep on the feather stuffed pillows on my bed. Her eyelids gently closed as her body rises and falls with steady breaths.

Elena Shen can even make sleeping look like an art form.

Like an idiot, I just sit there. My back against the headboard as I look down on the sleeping beauty beside me. It's hard to wrap my head around it. This amazing, beautiful, and talented woman is here...with me.

Her boyfriend.

Regardless of my wishes to stay in this moment for a lifetime, the sun still began its climb into the sky, and morning rang. I know the day ahead is going to be stressful, and I longed to bottle this moment up and save it for a rainy day.

I ever-so-gently slide myself out of bed, making sure she remains unbothered as I begin my morning routine. We only had a few hours until Aiko would be in the President's mansion.

After a quick shower and shave, I step out in my usual attire. Elena is already up and making tea.

"I hope I didn't wake you" I say, coming to wrap my arms tightly around her waist. My head sat nicely on her shoulder.

"No" She hums, turning the faucet on to fill up the kettle. "I didn't even notice you left"

"That's good" I say, moving to stand beside her. I notice her pick up the kettle and hesitate, eyes scanning the counter for a box of matches. "Here" I hum, taking the kettle in my left hand. With my right hand I flick my fingers, lips of flames rising and cradling the bottom of the kettle for a few seconds.

She looks at me with stunned eyes as I set the now steaming kettle on the counter.

"Well" She muses, "That is one way to do it"

"That is the firebender way to do it" I grin, reaching up to get two cups. "You know, I've never asked you this: Do you wish you were a bender?"

She licks her lips in thought, I can see her mind formulating the answer.

"When I was younger, yes, but not a lot. Since Vera isn't a bender I didn't feel jealous until Bo was born. Her abilities started to show very early and my parents gave her a lot of attention. I guess I grew out of it."

I nod, giving her a full cup of tea. "I always liked Waterbending. I thought it looked cool"

"I always admired Firebending" Elena replies, "Watching the Firebenders in the Fire Nation was incredible"

"I'd like to go there one day" I muse, leaning against the counter, "Maybe even get myself one of those cool red and black jackets you always see Fire Nation royalty wear"

"Shall we get you a crown while we are at it?" Elena grins playfully.

"I think that is necessary, yes" I joke back.

We spend the rest of the morning chatting and getting ready, our moods light. She spends some time at the piano while I wash the dishes from our meal. This feeling of domestication was something I could get used to.

A/N

Hi everyone! I thought I would give a nice fluffy update to you all. Am I the only one dying to see Mako and Elena together?! Also domesticated Mako is giving me so many feelings.

We are currently number ONE on the LegendOfKorra tag!! TT I can not believe it! Each day this story seems to grow and it is so exciting to see. I have been writing ahead and let me tell you- things are about to get interesting.

My favorite ATLA/LOK character is making their first appearance soon and I am SOOOO EXCITED. You guys are going to freak out.

I know it's Tuesday but I will still post a new chapter tomorrow. (TBH I wrote this one and couldn't wait to post it lol.)

Chapter 17

Spy Bug 100-

The room was elegant. Priceless vases and art pieces decorated the space. The far wall held large windows, the view overlooking the garden below. A butler had arranged two placemats, one at each end of the large wooden table that centered the room.

There was a potted plant that sat in the far corner- mostly forgotten by the guests. Hidden underneath a forest green leaf sat our little robotic spy, eyes glowing as eager ears listened from beyond.

A butler opened the large double doors. President Raiko entering first, followed by his guest, Aiko Nakamura. Aiko held his head high, his ego on his shoulders. He wore the finest of linens, a priceless gold belt clung to his hips.

Raiko nodded, excusing the butler from his duties as the meeting began. The door closed with a click, making Raiko's calm expression turn grim.

"This has gone too far, Aiko" He hissed, his eyebrows squeezed together.

Aiko sat back, his expression neutral. It was as if he was playing a tough game of Pai Sho.

"All in good time, my friend"

"Enough!" Raiko yelled, his fingers balling into a fist, "This has become a tabloid parade. The most well-known family in the world has been taken right under my nose. I am an embarrassment. How do you expect me to warrant respect from the people? From other leaders? I can't even keep a family safe."

"The Shen family is safe" Aiko counters, "They are fulfilling a special purpose"

Raiko scoffs, "And what is that purpose? Not getting me re-elected?"

"Raiko" Aiko says, leaning forward. "I understand your grief. So I will make you a deal-"

"I don't want another deal" Raiko spits, "I want this mess dealt with and the Shen's returned to their home"

"Easy now, my friend" Aiko says, a hand up in caution, "Do not reject proposals you have not yet heard"

President Raiko sits back in his chair, fingers tapping irritatedly against the tabletop. He was running out of patience.

"My colleague and I understand your time as leader will be coming to an end in the next year" Aiko begins, "We are prepared to offer you a large sum that could help you win this next election with ease"

Raiko raises an eyebrow in interest. "How much?"

"2 billion" Aiko grins.

Raiko scoffs, "That is absurd. I will not partake in meaningless bargaining"

Aiko reaches into his pocket and reveals a small tube filled with sparkling blue liquid. He sets it on the table with a small clink. Raiko's eyes tamed on the mysterious object.

"Do you see this serum?" Aiko says, eyes tamed on Raiko. "This serum is the most powerful thing on the planet. It has the power to turn back time. An old frail man could become as youthful as a child within minutes of ingesting it. Power like this is worth more than you and I can even comprehend. "

"Aiko" Raiko says flatly, "You are full of shit."

Aiko chuckles, pushing his chair away from the table. He stands, reaching into his coat pocket and brings out a small dead flower. Its stem is dark brown, the once beautiful flower now wilted. He opens up the bottle and drops a single droplet of serum onto the flower. Before their eyes it becomes green again, the shriveled stem becoming straight as the flower shows its beautiful pink color again.

The President was awe-struck, his mouth open in shock. His hand reaches out to take the flower, pulling it close to examine with his own eyes.

"Spirits" He swears under his breath, "This is amazing"

"The entire future can be changed with just one drop" Aiko says, putting the tube back in his coat. " Endless life, endless power"

"What do I have to do?" Raiko says, standing from his seat.

"Stay out of our way" Aiko says, "I need you to turn a blind eye. Can you continue to do that?"

"Yes" Raiko nods, "I can"

"Very well" Aiko says, "You will receive your payment shortly."

He gently bows his head to the President and turns, walking out of the room. Raiko sits back in chair, running a hand through his hair. His anxiety only grew.

-Mako-

The room was silent. All of us sat around a table in Asami's house while we listened to the radio relay the conversation between President Raiko and Aiko. Asami sighed, clicking the control off after we heard the sound of the doors closing.

Elena sat back in her seat, lip between her teeth. She was deep in thought.

My stomach was in knots. This entire situation was worse than what we expected.

The President was involved.

Everyone was eerily silent. Asami reached out to pat Elena softly on the back.

"We have to do something" Bolin says, "We have to go to the press and show the world that Raiko is not a good guy"

Korra stands, an intense look on her face.

"I will go and get the information out of him myself"

"He won't say anything" Elena sighs, looking up at Korra. "He is a stubborn and proud man. He won't cave"

"Then I'll beat it out of him" Korra corrects, tone cross.

"Korra, no" I say, grabbing her arm quickly to stop her, "We need to find out who is working with him- they might be keeping the Shens there"

Korra looks down at me with a neutral expression, nodding her head gently.

"So what's next?" Elena says, "Where do we go from here?"

"I have an idea" Asami says, then looks at me. "Mako, you won't like it"

"What is it?" I wince.

"The Benefit Recital" Asami says, "The plan Chief Beifong had before she was demoted."

"Absolutely not" I retort without a thought, "That is not happening." I can not believe we have to talk about this again.

"Mako" Elena says softly, reaching over to place her hand on mine. Korra's eyes shooting to look at me. "Please, I think this will work. We need to find out who he is working with."

"How do we even know they will be there?" I argue, folding my arms over my chest.

"We invite them" Asami shrugs, "Surely we can get enough wine in Tadashi that he'll tell us something."

"That," Elena points, "Could work. Tadashi is the type to have loose lips"

"Then it's settled," Asami says, clapping her hands. "The Benefit is back on!"

Chapter 18

I sigh, drawing mindless doodles on my notepad as the men around the room give their meaningless updates. Aiko sat at the desk, Tadashi standing quietly behind him with his hands resting in front of him.

Despite the news we heard yesterday, I still found myself playing Aiko's game and being present for all the 'updates' his men shared from their 'work' trying to find my family. It was boring, but we had to continue to let Aiko believe we didn't know anything wiser.

"Thank you, Hobi" Aiko nodded, "Please continue your search to bring my beloved friend and his family home"

"Yes sir" the man bowed then stepped back in line with the others.

I turned to Aiko, "Shall we break for lunch?"

"That is an excellent idea" Tadashi smiles, moving from his spot, "Let's go get lunch, El"

He excitedly took my arm, helping me stand. Without another glance to Aiko, he leads me out of the office and into the elevator.

"How are you holding up?" He asks, peering over at me.

"I'm doing alright" I reply, resisting the urge to roll my eyes. Why would he care? He's the one helping his father in this demonic scheme.

"That is good to hear" He nods, hand over his heart in false sincerity, "If there is anything you need, I am here for you"

"Thanks." I say flatly, turning my head forward as the elevator door rings.

We stroll for a few minutes in silence. My mind struggling to find a topic of conversation. All I wanted to do was yell at Tadashi. To scream at him. Has he no shame? That is my family he has taken from me.

"This place is delicious," Tadashi says, stopping in front of a small café.

I nod, following him inside. It was a Fire Nation themed café, the menu filled with Fire Nation cuisine. We sit at a table against the wall in the back, a server pouring us glasses of water.

"So" Tadashi says, folding his arms in front of me, "Who is this troublesome Firebender I see you with so much?"

I sip my water, gently placing it down on the table. I hold back a frown. Why would he care? He has proven he doesn't care about me. The man in front of me has betrayed me after years of friendship.

"A friend" I lie, licking my lips. "I met him when I moved here with my family"

Tadashi nods, sipping his own drink. I could see he was struggling to find a topic to talk about with me. Perhaps he was feeling guilty.

"How does Vera feel about that?" He asks, "With him being a Firebender and all"

I frown, my expression turning sour. How dare he talk about Vera.

"She likes him" I reply through gritted teeth.

"How did her and Iroh end?" He asks, mindlessly stirring his drink with his straw.

I did not want to talk about this.

"He became too busy" I say, careful not to say too much. "It was before we left the Fire Nation"

"That is too bad" Tadashi frowns, "I remember how much he loved her"

I nod, trying to suppress the memories.

Vera was heartbroken. She didn't eat for days after. Iroh was truly the love of her life. That breakup effected the entire family.

"Tadashi, why did you come here?" I say freely, fed up with the pointless small talk.

He looks up at me in shock, like he had just been caught. "Because you are my friend, and you needed me"

"I didn't need you" I retort angrily. "You simply showed up with your father and ruined everything we had set in place."

Tadashi stares at me in shock, mouth slack. "My father is the smartest man I know, he is going to save your family. Chief Beifong and that moronic Firebender of yours couldn't save a fly from a frog."

I stand, blood boiling. "You are half the man Mako is" I hiss, "We would all be better off with you and your slimy father out of this city."

"Elena, you don't know what you are saying" Tadashi frowns, his tone calm, "You are working too hard, it must be tiresome for you."

I scoff, rolling my eyes. If I don't leave soon, I will say something that could hurt this entire plan. Get it together Elena. I inhale a deep breath into my lung, well aware of Tadashi's slimy eyes on me.

I inhale sharply though my nose. "You're right" I lie, "I must be feeling the effects of this whole thing. I'm sorry"

Tadashi gives me a toothless smile, reaching up to pat my arm gingerly.

"It's okay, Elena" He says, a false sense of sincerity in his voice. "I am here to help"

-Mako -

I groan, rubbing my hands over my face in frustration. Asami had set up a meeting with the organizers of the Benefit Recital so Korra and I can review their safety measures. All would have been swell if Korra hadn't been so sour the entire time.

"And this is the dressing room Miss Shen would use" An older woman says, gesturing to a closed door. "There is no other exit from this room, only a small window that doesn't open."

I nod, my hands clasped behind my back.

"Do you think that will be good enough for Miss Shen?" Korra asks, her tone taunting.

My blood boils, heat gathering in my palms. I had had enough.

"Will you excuse us, please?" I say to the woman, quickly grabbing Korra's arm and leading her down the hall and into the empty stairwell of the auditorium.

"Okay, what the fuck is your problem?" I hiss, trying to keep my voice down.

"I don't know what you are talking about" Korra says plainly, crossing her arms over her chest, playing coy.

I roll my eyes, "Cut the crap, Korra" I bark, "You have been acting like a brat all day. What is your problem?"

"I don't know, Mako" She fights back, "Maybe it is because you lied to me!"

"Lied to you?" I shrill, "What in the spirits are you talking about?"

"I asked you point blank who the new girl you were interested in was" Korra barks, "You did not tell me it was little miss rich girl"

"First of all, I told you that I would not tell you because I didn't feel comfortable" I correct, "and second, why does it matter?"

"It matters because this is the girl we are trying to protect!" Korra yelps, "She is a target! We are working our assess off to protect her and find her snobby little family all the while you are sleeping with her"

"We aren't sleeping together" I bark back, my anger growing. Out of the corner of my eye I see our tour guide turn away, trying to not listen to our argument. "Even if we were, why does that matter? I like her! We are dating. I can still protect her if she was or was not my girlfriend"

Korra's face morphs into a frown. "She's your girlfriend?"

"Yes" I sigh, fed up. "Yes, she is. And I really like her. I want to protect her and find her family while enjoying her company. Is that a crime?"

"No" She sighs, running a hand through her hair, "Fuck, I don't know."

She sits down on the stair step, head in her hands in defeat.

"I guess I'm just shocked," Korra confesses, her voice uneasy. "I'm still working through these feelings and I didn't expect you to just... move on"

I sit beside her, my anger fading into empathy.

"I know" I say, "You and I are just two very different people."

"Extremely" Korra chuckles in agreement. "Some might say polar opposites"

I nod, a small smile on my face, "Exactly" I say. "And I know it feels weird for you but I really like Elena. I think she is something special"

She nods, a faint smile on her lips. Korra opens her mouth to say something, only to close it a second later. The awkward air between us only rose. After a moment I stand, hands shoved into my pockets.

"We should get back to the tour"

She nods, slowly standing from the stair steps. I watch her carefully, as if she might explode into a fiery ball of anger at any moment. Knowing Korra, she just might.

-

I sigh, turning off the engine in my police kart. I am exhausted. I reach for my small bag and get out, locking my kart before heading inside my apartment building.

What a day. Between the stress of the Benefit and Korra's childish outburst, I felt like I had been through a war. I drag my feet down the hallway and to my front door.

Faint voices can be heard on the other side as I shove the the key in the lock and turn the doorknob.

Elena sits on the couch with a dark haired man, I faintly recognize his voice. Elena turns and smiles at me as I kick off my shoes.

"Mako" she smiles, "Look who is here!"

I look up and see Iroh standing, a smile on his face. "Long time no see, Mako"

A/N:

IROH HAS ARRIVED!! I can't wait for you all to see what I have planned!

Chapter 19

Mako-

In a way, I have always admired Iroh. Growing up, I always assumed children that came from such a status like him would grow up to be assholes. Iroh, certainly did not. He is a genuinely caring person and a damn good bender- which I appreciated.

I knew he cared greatly for Elena and her family, mostly because of her sister, Vera. Whatever his reasoning may be, I was glad to have another person to help us out.

"Thank you for coming" I said, reaching out to shake his hand.

He returned the gesture, squeezing my fingers endearingly. "It's a shame the reasoning, but I am more than happy to help."

"This would mean the world to Vera" Elena says, a small sad smile on her lips.

Iroh frowns, shoving his hands into the pockets of his trousers. "I know. It breaks my heart that she and the family are in danger. I will do whatever I can"

"We have a few ideas" I say, glancing at Vera, "We are planning to attend this fancy party this weekend. A lot of notable people will be there. We are hoping to catch someone in the act"

"Elena told me about Riako" Iroh frowns, "I'm pissed. I already sent a radio message back home"

"Do you think the Fire Nation would be willing to help us?" Elena asks, "Clearly the leadership here is no use"

"I bet we'll be able to do something" Iroh assures us, "I don't know what that is right now, but once I hear back from my mother I will let you know. My grandfather was so upset when he heard the news"

"My parents care greatly for the Fire Lord" Elena frowns, "Anything they can do will be met with much gratitude"

I shove my hands in my pockets, watching the two high-born people talk about their high-born families. I feel a little dumb, standing there without any political status. I didn't have a family that could send countless soldiers, or millions of yuans to throw at the situation. I just have myself and my bending.

"Mako has been a hero" Elena chimes in, reaching over to squeeze my arm gently.

Iroh gives me a proud smirk, "That is the type of attitude we could use in the United Forces"

I shrug, writing his compliment off to niceties, "Thanks"

"Well" Elena says, clasping her hands together, "I'm sure you are hungry from your journey, shall we get something to eat?"

"Great idea" Iroh says, "I'm starving."

The night had just begun when we all arrived at Koda's. Asami gives a quick smile to the hostess and we are escorted back into a private dining room. I sit down beside Elena at the head of the table. To my right is Bolin, followed by Asami, Korra, and finally Iroh on Elena's otherside.

"Too bad this place has a rule against pets" Bolin frowns, glancing over the menu, "Pabu would love this place"

"Bring him some takeaway fried squid and noodles" Asami suggests, glancing over the menu. "Does he like squid?"

"Pabu will eat anything" I add, "Literally. One time I saw him eat right out of the garbage can"

Everyone chuckles, Bolin looking at me with a scoff, "He was eating leftovers!"

A waiter comes and serves us drinks followed by an assortment of appetizers. Asami coordinates a few more items to be brought out for the table as we begin our feast.

"So this Benefit Recital" Iroh says, sipping from his glass, "What is it?"

"The Republic City Conversatory of Music is hosting a benefit recital for the local schools this weekend." Elena explains, "I was invited to perform when I first moved here. After my family was taken it was reschedule until now"

"Aiko and President Raiko will be there?" Iroh asks, looking around the table.

"Yes" Korra answers, picking up a dumpling, "We believe we might be able to get some information out of Aiko or his moronic son."

"Asami and Bolin will talk to the attendees while I play in hopes to gain some insight. Mako and Korra will be outside as security to make sure no one tries to kill me" Elena says, making me swallow hard.

"So, where do you want me?" Iroh asks, "Security?"

"I can use another Firebender on my side" I say, giving him a friendly smile.

"With you three, we'll be lucky if the whole auditrom doesn't burn down" Asami chuckles.

Iroh laughs, leaning back in his seat, "I just hope I don't get caught between any lover's spats"

I freeze, eyes shooting to Korra who sat on the other end of the table. She swallows hard, avoiding my gaze.

He doesn't know we broke up.

"I don't think that will be a problem" I say, clearing my throat. "Korra and I aren't together anymore"

I can feel the awkwardness in the air as I reach up and adjust the collar of my shirt. Elena glances over and gives me a warm smile, clearly understanding the mishap. What an angel.

I reach up to bring the cup of wine to my lips, taking a sip.

"Really?" Iroh asks, clearly shocked, "I must say, I'm surprised"

"I'm not" Korra hums, effortlessly moving the items on her plate around. "Mako can't seem to keep it in his pants."

My eyes widen, quickly inhaling in surprise. I cough, my hand going to my chest to help regain composure. What the fu-

"Actually, Mako and I are dating," Elena announces to the table, a smile spreading across her lips. "He asked me a few days ago. He has been nothing short of a perfect gentleman."

Asami glances at me nervously, clearly thinking the same thing I was.

They are about to go at it.

-Elena -

I am not the type of person to stoop to someone's level. I find it to be immature and frankly counter-intuitive. But for some reason, Korra's outburst really got under my skin. What was her problem? Isn't the Avatar supposed to be nice all the time? Bring peace or something?

Iroh turns to me, a genuine smile on his lips, "Well, little El is all grown up. Congratulations to the both of you"

I smile, my hand reaching under the table to settle on Mako's knee. I could tell Korra's outburst had rocked him. His golden eyes meet mine and he mimics my smile, his hand clasping mine on his knee.

Bolin starts on another topic as I take another bite of my food. I can feel Korra's eyes on me as I eat, the little hairs on my arms sticking up. I can't show her that I am affected.

After a few minutes Korra excuses herself to go to the washroom, scooting back from the table. We watch her go, the dining room door closing with a click.

"I'm going to see what that was all about" Mako says to me, leaning over to peck my cheek gently.

"Don't let her beat you up" Bolin teases, a grin on his face.

I give him a reassuring smile and watch him go, the door closing again.

"I'm sorry about her" Asami frowns, "She hasn't taken the news lightly."

I nod, biting the inside of my cheek. Of course it was awkward, and I hated to be the cause of it. But I'm not going to withhold my feelings just to make her happy. That isn't fair.

"She's a good person" Bolin says, "A great person, even. She just cares a lot for Mako. It's going to take some time for her to get over things."

"I understand," I say, "I don't want her to see me as an enemy."

"She's young," Iroh says, "Even though she has these incredible gifts and is the Avatar, she is still just a twenty year old girl. She will mature, it takes time. When I was twenty I was a complete fool."

I laugh lightly, "When you were twenty you were in love with Vera"

Iroh nods, his expression changing. "Who said I ever stopped?"

Bolin and Asami harmonize in an array of adoring comments. I was mostly thrilled to hear that he still loved Vera. But part of me was sad. If she were here they could be together again.

"Firebenders are such romantics" Asami comments, sipping her drink cooly.

"I saw a study that Earthbenders are more likely to have divorces" Bolin adds, beforing diving into conversation with Asami and Iroh.

I space out, curious as to what Mako and Korra might be saying. I quietly slide my chair back, deciding I was going to go see for myself.

The doors of our room open and close behind me, the group so enthralled by their conversation they don't even notice I'm gone. I turn down a hallway leading toward the kitchen, their voices echoing off the walls.

"You are being ridiculous" I hear Mako bite.

"I am not!" Korra replies, " I don't think it's right."

"Why?" He argues, "I like her! I don't see how my feelings for her are so wrong."

"We have to protect her, Mako" Korra says, "Don't you think your feelings will affect the way we do our job?"

"No" Mako says confidently. "If anything, my feelings for her want me to protect her even more."

"You don't understand what I am saying, Mako" Korra sighs, "Have you told her the truth? Or are you sugar-coating this entire situation to make her feel better? We both know it isn't likely we will find her family. It's been weeks and we have no leads to where they are."

"Of course I'm not going to say that to her, Korra" He groans, "It's important we remain positive"

"Mako, I saw her apartment after they were taken. Whoever took them is powerful and dangerous. Her family is gone."

I step back, my back leaning against the wall. I feel as though a pile of bricks had been set on my shoulders. Was my family really gone?

Chapter 20

I t was raining outside. The droplets of water felt good on my skin. I felt as though the rain was a fair attempt to calm my pumping nerves. I grip the wall outside the restaurant, a pool of water at my feet reflecting the light above the door. Everyone was still inside enjoying their night. After overhearing Mako and Korra's conversation, I ran outside for some air.

I grip the collar of my dress, monitoring my breathing to try and calm myself down. I know I'm on the edge of a full-blown panic attack. Each little drop of rain that lands on my skin only makes it worse. They played a hurtful reminder that my family is most likely dead.

I inhale sharply, my eyes blurring with tears as I reach out into the night air, letting the rain collect in my palm. My mind replays the memories of my mother and Bo bending, their hands fluid as the water dances around them.

I frown, hiccuping as tears roll down my checks and drop my hand to my side.

I can't bend. I can't find my family. I am useless.

The echo of voices bounces around me, people running past me quickly with their umbrella clinging in their fingers. I envied them. I envied their happiness- their joy. I bet their family wasn't missing.

"Practicing your waterbending?"

I turn, pieces of hair sticking to my face. I squint to see Mako standing there, the stem of a black umbrella in his hand.

I scoff, "I'm not in the mood"

"You should come inside" Mako says, eyes wandering over me worriedly, "You'll catch a cold"

"Good" I say dramatically, "Perhaps the cold will kill me"

Mako frowns, his expression turning grim, "Elena, do not say things like that"

"Why?" I scoff, "Because you want me to sugar-coat things? Like you have been this entire time? You made me look like a fool, prancing around with this false sense of hope. Why didn't you tell me the truth? That my family is dead?"

"Elena" Mako says, inhaling quickly, "We don't know that for sure."

"Korra sure thinks so" I retort, "She's the Avatar"

"Korra is a lot of things" Mako replies, "She can be brutally candid some-times. But she isn't always right, just like how she isn't right about your parents"

"Come on, Mako" I roll my eyes, tears mixing with the rain drops on my face. "I'm not a child. Please just be honest with me."

"I am" He pleads, "Elena, I promised you I would find them and I mean it"

I lick my lips, trying to find something to say. I'm mentally exhausted.

"I know you're scared, but I know in my heart that things are going to be okay. I have never been so sure of something my entire life" Mako confesses, "I just need you to trust me."

"Mako.." I sigh, reaching up to wipe my eyes.

"Really, Elena." He says, reaching up to grab my hand. "I will do anything on this planet to find them. If you want me to walk to every village and search under every rock, I will. That's how much I care about you"

I just look at him, overwhelmed with emotion. Another sob escapes my lips, Mako dropping the umbrella and using both arms to wrap me into his chest. The heat from his body feels warm against my chilled skin, my clothes soaked with water.

"I'm sorry you heard us talking" Mako mumbles, his face in my hair.

I hug him tighter in response, letting him nuzzle deeping into me.

"This is becoming too much" I confess, feeling my emotions boil over. "All of it. Tadashi, my family, Korra, you."

Mako frowns, his eyes falling to the soaked pavement. I could see the guilt in his face- he felt terrible.

"What can I do to make it up to you?" He says, voice pleading. "You mean the world to me, Elena. I want you to be happy. I want to be the guy that solves your problems and saves the day. I can't stand seeing you like this"

My fingers run through my hair, my nails scratching my scalp. I know I'm not in a good place. I could practically feel my anxiety in my veins.

"I don't know" I sigh, my hands dropping to my sides. "I care about you, Mako. But you have to be honest with me-"

"-and I need you to trust me," Mako interrupts. "I would never lie to you."

I nod, I held no more energy to talk about it anymore.

"We should go back inside" I say, reaching up to wipe my eyes with the back of my hand. Mako steps forward, wrapping me in his arms. I feel the heat from his body against mine, the warmth feeling nice from the cold rain.

I feel him place a kiss on top of my head, his voice a low murmur: "We will get through this"

Will we?

-Mako-

I slid back into the seat at the table, the rest of the group engrossed in a conversation. Elena sits down softly, her eyes still red from crying. I nervously glance at her, praying no one comments about it.

"Everything alright?" Iroh asks, a glass between his fingers.

"All good" I reply diplomatically, giving him a small nod. He blinks, the look on his face clearing saying he doesn't believe me.

"I think we picked out Elena's gown for the recital" Asami says, turning to smile at her. "She looks beautiful in it"

I grin, "I'm looking forward to seeing it"

I know she'll look stunning. She could make a brown bag look beautiful.

"Asami was so kind and let me raid her closet" Elena chuckles, "She has an entire department store in there"

"I believe it" Bolin says, "Ginger has a giant closet too. Pabu got lost in it once"

"Bolin" Iroh says, "Is it true you and Ginger are a thing?"

I roll my eyes, "No" I say, "Bolin just wants them to be"

"Now wait a second" Bolin defends, his hand raised. "Mako doesn't see the connection Ginger and I share. It's some pretty serious stuff"

"The only connection you have is with ramen" I tease, making the group laugh.

Bolin starts on a rant to defend himself while I sit back, zoning out.

I know in my heart Elena's family is safe. But maybe Korra is right. The damage done in the family's apartment was incredibly grim. Even the most optimistic people have to admit there is a fair chance they are dead.

I shouldn't think that way. I have to remain positive. For Elena.

Chapter 21

"I 'm sorry, can we start over?"

I sit at my piano on the center stage at the conservatory. Today was our final rehearsal before the big night. Stagehands littered the area as our director made sure all our cues were timed correctly.

"Sure" Minnie, our director says. She turns to face the man running the spotlight. "We are starting from the top!"

Mako watches from backstage, his arms crossed over his chest. He had been with me at every rehearsal making sure everything was going according to plan. Korra and Iroh were outside making sure they knew exactly what their plan was.

The spot light turns on and I'm bathed in the golden glow. I exhale gently before placing my fingers on the keys and starting my song. I get through a few bars before my finger slips and I press the wrong key.

I huff, lifting my hands from the keys and moving my foot from the pedal. The tune stops abruptly, echoing around the theater.

"It's okay" Minnie says from below, "Take your time. You are a magnificent musician, you can do this"

I inhale sharply, trying to relax my nerves. This was the fifth time I had messed up. I had yet to be able to get through the entire piece.

"Do you need a moment, Elena?" Minnie asks.

"No" I reply, not looking at her. "I can do it"

"Alright" she says, less convinced. Then turns to the spot light technician, "Restart!"

"You got this, El" Mako calls.

I close my eyes, taking a deep breath before opening them again and raising my hands to the keys. My fingers begin to move as the song plays. I lean myself closer to the piano as I feel the music flow through me. It was an intoxicating feeling. As soon as I felt I was hitting my stride, my mind blanked and I forgot the next cord.

Cheeks red, I lift my fingers from the keys and hang my head low.

"I'm sorry" I say, my vision clouded with tears, "I don't know what is wrong with me"

Minnie frowns, quickly walking up the stairs and across the stage toward me. I hear the murmurs of the stagehands as I watch them with tears running down my cheeks. Minnie stands beside me, placing a hand on my shoulder.

"Are you okay?" She asks, a worried look on her face.

"I just- I just need a minute." I say, reaching up to wipe a tear from my eye. I see Mako walking up, his face echoing the same look of concern as Minnie.

"Let's take five, everyone" Minnie announces, then turns back to me. "Take as much time as you need, Elena."

I nod, mumbling a 'Thanks' before standing from my seat. I wrap my arms around myself as I walk off the stage, Mako a few steps behind me.

"Do you need some water?" He asks, watching me lean against the brick wall backstage.

"No" I sigh, looking up at the rafters on the ceiling, "I am just nervous.. I guess.. I don't know"

Mako frowns, moving to lean against the wall beside me. "Like.. nervous for the show?"

"For everything" I confess. "I haven't played in front of a crowd since I moved here, and I know there is a chance someone could come to the show to try and hurt me. I know everyone will be there to protect me but it's just... nerve wracking to think about"

"I understand," Mako says calmly, "You are under a lot of pressure. We can cancel if you want"

I shake my head, "No, we can't. Too much is on the line. This might be the last chance we get to get some information about my parents."

"There will be other opportunities," Mako says, looking at me seriously, "This isn't the end."

I press my lips together. I knew he was wrong. It was obvious tomorrow night is a golden opportunity to find out information from Aiko and Tadashi. Too many powerful people are going to be in attendance for us to miss out on such a chance.

I inhale deeply, trying to calm my fast-beating heart. "I can do this"

"Yes, you can" Mako says. "You can do it"

I nod, shaking my hands in an attempt to get rid of the access nerves as I walk back toward the stage. I can do this

- Mako -

I could watch her play piano all day. It comes so naturally to her. The way her entire body moves and flows with the music is so amazing to watch. It was like she was painting a beautiful painting with music notes.

I stand backstage watching her in awe. After our quick pep-talk she was able to go through the entire song and hit every note perfectly. I clapped hard as she grinned, a look of relief on her face. Minnie was relieved and asked if she could do it one more time so they could finalize the lighting cues.

Iroh stands beside me, hands in his pockets as he watches her.

"She's great, isn't she?" I say, my voice laced with affection.

"She's incredible," Iroh agrees. "I remember when she played for my family. The entire palace came to watch her- she is a natural."

"It's amazing" I smile.

"I heard you gave her a good pep-talk," Iroh says, glancing sideways at me. "She really likes you, doesn't she?"

I shrug, a small blush growing on my cheeks.

"I mean... I hope" I say, scratching the back of my neck, "I care about her a lot"

"I can tell" Iroh says, a small smile on his lips. "I've known Elena for a long time, I know how she can get when she is nervous. I've never seen someone be able to calm her down so quickly. Not even Vera."

I raise an eyebrow, "Really?"

"Yeah" Iroh confirms, "It is beautiful to watch, you two are clearly falling in love"

Love? Could Elena really love me?

My entire body felt warm at the thought. The fact that this beautiful, brilliant, and talented woman could fall in love with me? Elena Shen, of THE Shen family.... In love with me?

"I guess we are" I say, a small smile breaking on my face. Iroh chuckles, giving me a reassuring pat on the shoulder before walking away.

Back in her dressing room a few people are talking to her about details about the show. I stand against the wall and half listen. My mind running in circles from what Iroh mentioned earlier. After a few minutes the people bid their farewells and we are left alone.

I look at her through her reflection in the wall sized mirror she sat in front of, her lips breaking into a smile.

"Did you like the song?" she asks

"I loved it" I reply, "You wrote it, right?"

She nods, setting her elbows on the counter and putting her head in her hands. "It's called A Glow in the Night"

"That sounds poetic" I muse, a goofy smile on my face.

She shrugs her shoulders lightly, "I wrote it the day you gifted me the piano. It really inspired me"

"I'm glad" I say, "You did an incredible job"

Her eyes flicker to my lips, then quickly flashing over my body. Heat fills my cheeks as I visibly watch her check me out. Deciding to be cheeky, I smirk and say:

"Miss Shen, did I just catch you checking me out?" I grin, stepping toward her so I am standing right behind her.

Her mouth falls open in shock, cheeks flushed pink. She doesn't say anything, her lips pressed together. I could tell she was trying to keep a straight face.

"Well?" I prod, eyebrow raised, "Were you?"

"What if I was?" She retorts, her tone playful.

I reach out and brush my fingers on the skin of her neck gently, my fingertips just glazing her skin. I could feel her body move slightly in response, her chest moving as she inhaled sharply. I remain silent as I slowly move my fingers up and down her skin, watching how she reacts.

The sleeve of her dress sat on her shoulder, my fingers scooping under the material and pushing it away, watching her smooth skin reveal itself below. I hear her inhale sharply again, her eyes hooded as she watches me in the reflection of the mirror.

"You are so fucking beautiful" I murmur, locking eyes with her in the mirror.

I watch her gulp and blink slowly- clearly my actions were getting to her.

"So are you" she replies, her voice sounding out of breath. "I like it when you do that"

"Do what?" I say, still mindlessly moving my fingers up and down her arm and shoulder.

"Touch me" She replies, "I like it when you touch me"

"Why?" I say, begging to hear her say more.

"Because it makes me feel good" She says, "I can't describe it"

"Try" I almost demand, feeling my nerves turn electric.

She is quiet for a moment, visibly thinking. I turn and begin to rub her other shoulder, pushing the sleeve of her dress down her arm again. Now her upper chest was exposed to me, her collarbone smooth under her skin. It was intoxicating.

"It feels like my skin is warm- hot even" she thinks aloud, "I've never felt this way before- I feel it all through my body"

"You're turned on" I conclude, "Is that it?"

She hums in reply, almost as if she is too embarrassed to admit it aloud.

"You turn me on" I say freely, watching her intently. "You turn me on more than anyone"

She slowly reaches up and places her hand over mine, gripping my fingers tightly. I feel her move my hand and place it over her left breast. The fabric of her dress half-covered her chest.

Wordlessly she removes her hand from mine, allowing me to free-roam. My head was spinning. Her breast fit perfectly in my hand. I squeeze it once, hearing her gasp below me. I watch her intently as I do it again, and again. Eventually the fabric of her dress is shoved lower and I see her full chest on display.

"You are so fucking hot" I say, feeling myself groan, my hands continuing to explore.

Right as I am about to lift her up out of her chair there is a knock on the door. I jump back in surprise, watching her quickly fix her dress.

"Yes?" She calls, cheeks still flushed.

"Elena, we need you to approve one last item" Minnie calls from the other side of the door.

"Be there in a second" she calls, standing and smoothing out her gown.

She gives me a quick smile as she leaves, closing the door behind her. I am left leaning against the wall; horny and totally, utterly, and completely stunned by the gorgeous woman Elena Shen was.

Chapter 22

I sit in front of a mirror in my dressing room. The entire tabletop was littered with make up, hair products, and various other cosmetic items. Asami stood behind me, rolling curlers into my hair.

Tonight was the night of the big show. I could feel the butterflies in my stomach. I had been unable to sleep all night last night, my mind reeling at the events that could unfold. What if something bad happened?

"Stop thinking so hard" Asami says, a small smile on her face. I blink, looking up at her in the mirror.

"How did you know I was thinking?"

"You get this super intense look on your face" Asami replies, picking up a hair brush.

"Oh" I say dumbly, "I didn't know I did that"

"Well, regardless, don't overthink things" Asami says, "Everything is under control. All you have to do is look beautiful and play your song"

"I guess" I sigh, looking down at my hands. "I just.. Can't stop thinking about it"

"Then let's talk about something else" Asami offers, the pauses, "How are you and Mako?"

I instantly blush, flashbacks of yesterday flowing through my mind. It had been so intense and....sexy. It was the most intense moment I had ever had with someone.

"We are good" I reply, trying to keep my cool.

Asami chuckles, glancing up at me with an eyebrow rasied. "Spill."

"What?"

"Spill!" She repeats, "You are clearly keeping something juicy from me"

I think for a moment, trying to decide how to frame what I wanted to say. She brushes another strand of my hair and begins to roll it into a curler.

"Mako and I had this..." I pause, "We had this really heated moment last night"

She looks at me intrigued, "Continue"

"I don't know" I say, fumbling over my words. "We just had this moment where we just.. Looked deep into eachothers eyes and he was touching my neck really softly and... I don't know how to explain it."

"Did you guys have sex?" Asami asks bluntly, making me blush.

"Oh, no" I say quickly, "No. We aren't there yet"

"Do you want to?" Asami asks

I nod, "I do, when the time is right."

She nods, humming in agreement. "I think that is a good idea. It is never good to rush things like that"

"Have you ever had sex?" I ask out of curiosity.

Asami was the drop-dead gorgeous type, I was almost positive she had.

She nods, "I have."

"What was it like?" I ask, my mind was dying to know.

Vera and I never talked about such taboo things. I figured Vera and Iroh had consummated their relationship, but I was always too shy to ask, nor was Vera the type to offer up such intimate details.

"It's fun" Asami says after a moment, "But only when you are relaxed and feeling good about yourself. The worst thing you can do is overthink it and psyche yourself out."

Then a question popped into my mind, making my heart race.

"Did you and Mako ever...."

"No" Asami says calmly, sensing my nerves. "I wasn't ready when we were together. He was really understanding about it."

"That is good" I say, "I mean, good that he was understanding, not that you didn't have sex- but I mean, I am sort of glad you guys didn't. You know, because we are together and you're my friend" I ramble, a flush climbing on my cheeks

"Relax, El" Asami chuckles, "Sex is a natural thing that happens when two people feel attraction toward each other. There is nothing to be embarrassed about."

"It's just hard not to be" I confess, "It is so... revealing"

"Sometimes it is nice to be with someone on such an intimate level," Asami says, picking up a bottle of hairspray.

"I guess" I say, unsure.

In all honesty- I was terrified. I didn't know the first thing about being sexually intimate with someone.

"The best advice I can give is to relax and be yourself" Asami says, "And to speak up, don't be scared to speak up and say what you do and don't enjoy. Sex is for him and you."

I give her a small smile, "Thanks, Asami."

"Anytime" She replies, setting her hands on my shoulders. "I think you are ready!"

My hair was curled down my back, the middle pieces pinned up. The curls Asami created rolled down my back beautifully. My make up was light, my eyes a light shade of pink and cheeks rosy.

"You are an artist" I compliment. I hadn't felt this good in a while.

"Comes from years of practice" Asami grins, "Now go get ready!"

About 20 minutes later I sat in my dressing room with Asami and a few stagehands. The show was starting in less than an hour. I had done my warm ups and did a quick run through before the Conservatory doors opened to the guests.

I sat in a chair in my silk-pink dress that fell to my feet, my eyes gazing over the crumpled sheet of music I had carried with me for weeks. There is a knock on the door, making me look up.

The door opens and Tadashi pokes his head in, making my nerves pump quickly.

"Hey! Mind if we stop in?" He says, a wide grin on his face.

"Sure" I sit up, swallowing hard. I give Asami a quick glance.

Tadashi pushes the door open more and he steps inside. He wore a forest green suit with a bow-tie. His hair looked like it had a million layers of gel on it.

Following behind him was a woman with pale white skin and jet black hair that was pinned perfectly on her head. Her eyes were a golden colored brown- almost like Mako's. Her dress was blood-red with a slit cut up to her lower thigh. She stood beside Tadashi, her shoulders back with a stern look on her face.

"How are you feeling? Nervous?" Tadashi asks, making me break my gaze from the woman.

"Yea" I reply, "I hope I don't forget the notes or something"

"You are a professional, El. You will do great!" Tadashi says, then turns to the woman he came with. "El, this is my friend, Lillian."

I stand from my seat, giving the woman a bow. I look up to see her standing straight, a cold looking smirk on her face.

Did she not bow?

"It is a pleasure to meet you, Lillian," I say kindly, caught-off guard. She only looks down thoughtlessly at her nails, as if I wasn't even there.

"Um" I hesitated, "Where did you meet?"

"A mutual friend" Tadashi replies happily. He was acting as if he had no idea how rude this woman was being.

"His father introduced us," the woman says, meeting my gaze. Her voice was chilling, it made the hairs on my arms stick up. Her tone and demeanor was almost.. Sinister.

"I hope you enjoy the show" I say, praying this awkward interaction would end soon.

"We'll meet you afterwards" Tadashi suggests, "I am hosting an after-party! You should totally come."

"Sounds lovely" I rush, walking with them to the door. "I'll let you know, goodbye"

I shut the door behind them, leaning against it.

"That girl was freaky" Asami points, leaning back in her seat. "Like- she might be an evil spirit"

"I wouldn't put it past Tadashi and his father" I sigh. "I could feel her eyes sinking into my soul"

"Exactly" Asami says, a distraught look on her face, "But that doesn't matter, you just need to focus on tonight"

I lift my thumb and pinch my nail with my teeth nervously. But Asami was right, that isn't important right now. I have to focus. This is it.

Chapter 23

- -

Mako -

The air was chilly that night, the wind whipping off the sea a few blocks away. I lean against the brick on the outside of the venue, Korra a few paces away. We glance at each other now and then, almost as if to make sure the other person wasn't coming over to talk.

We had been wary of each other since the night at Koda's.

Not like that was my fault. She was the one that blew up at me.

Iroh was stationed at the other entrance, our garments black, to blend in. Part of me was dying to see Elena and wish her a good show. But I knew my place was here.

It was only a few minutes until the show began, and President Raiko and Aiko had not shown. I was starting to suspect they simply weren't going to come. Which would be a positive if it wasn't for the fact they could be avoiding a potentially dangerous situation.

I stayed silent, my eyes scanning the almost empty sidewalk in front of me. A few moments pass before I feel someone stand beside me.

"I haven't seen anything suspicious" Iroh comments, arms crossed in front of his chest.

"Me neither" I reply, "I saw Tadashi come in, that is it. It's just a bunch of rich people"

"Who was the girl he was with?" Iroh asks, "I feel like I know her from somewhere"

I shrug, "Never seen her before. We will keep an eye on them."

"She could be... you know..." Iroh teases, "Paid company"

I chuckle, "You think so?"

"I wouldn't be shocked," Iroh smirks.

Right as I am about to come up with another joke Korra walks up, a bored look on her face.

"They aren't coming. The show starts in like 10 minutes." She complains.

"We still need to be prepared for anything" I warn, "They might be keeping their distance from a fight"

"Who is going to fight us? Aiko's moronic son?" Korra snorts, "I could snap him in half like a twig"

"I would like to see you do that" Iroh notes, an amused look on his face.

"Regardless" I say, trying to get us back on topic, "We need to keep a close eye. I don't have a good feeling"

Korra huffs, mumbling something under her breath. I scan the space outside before turning to them, "We should go inside"

Iroh and Korra nod, wordlessly following me into the theater. Almost everyone was inside and seated, the show starting within minutes. I stand in the back, my arms crossed over my chest as I scan the crowd. A few notable people sit in the baloney seats. Ginger sat beside Bolin, followed by a few more famous figures. Across the theater was Tadashi and his date, both sitting side by side in their own balcony overlooking the stage. The woman had a stern look on her face, a paper fan flapping in her fingers.

I kept my gaze on them as the lights went out and applause roared. A single spot light lit up on center stage as Minnie made her way to the microphone.

"Good Evening, everyone" She smiled. Minnie was older, probably within her late 40s. She was a career musician that came from a long line of Earthbenders. "My name is Minnie, and I am the Director of Fine Arts here at the Republic City Conversatory of Music. I am so excited to welcome you all here tonight. This is the biggest night in music education, as all the funds raised here will help students find their love of music-"

I feel Iroh slide over next to me, leaning in to whisper: "Three bulky Firebenders a few rows to the left. The keep looking up at Tadashi"

"You think it's trouble?" I reply, eyebrow raised.

He shrugs, "Better keep an eye on them"

"I am pleased to introduce our first performer. She is a piano player hailing from the famous Waterbending Shen family. In recent times she has been struck with tragedy since her family's disappearance, but she is here tonight to play an original song called, A Glow in the Night. Please welcome, Elena Shen"

I hear the room burst into applause as the spotlight goes out on Minnie and moves to the grand piano on the left side of the stage. Elena sits in a vibrant pink gown, her hair curled down her shoulders. I could feel my mouth drop- she looked stunning.

After a moment, she reaches her hands up and strikes the first note. Even though I had heard the song countless times, watching her play made it feel like it was the first time. The way each chord was played so brilliantly, it was like the music was swirling around her. Everyone in the room was captivated by her beauty and talent.

It was like watching a beautiful sunset on the beach.

The climax of the song hit and I was stunned, watching her quickly move her fingers up and down the keys, shoulders moving and head bouncing gently to the tempo. It was as if her entire body was an extension of the piano.

To my dismay, the song ended. I watched adoringly as the entire theater rose to their feet and clapped. She stood and bowed, a gleam in her eye as she watched hundreds of people give her their applause. She bowed once more before exiting, the crowd seeming to settle down as Minnie appeared to introduce the next guest.

I glanced up and noticed Tadashi and his guest were not in their balcony anymore. Without a thought I dart out of the theater and head backstage.

-Elena -

A few stagehands backstage give me their congratulations. I happily thank them, the adrenaline running through my veins. Asami waits in the wing, wrapping her arms around me.

"My Spirits!" she exclaims, "You were brilliant- no, better than brilliant, you were perfect!"

I grin, hugging her back tightly. "I was so nervous"

"You couldn't even tell" she says, pulling away. "The entire room was completely transfixed by you"

"It felt good" I say, running a hand through my hair. "I felt like it was good"

"It was incredible" Minnie smiles, the sound of the next pianist's song echoing around us. "I am so proud"

"Thank you Minnie" I say, hugging her, "This was much needed"

"We are happy to have you, Elena" She smiles, "We would love to have you come teach here at the conservatory, if you like?"

My eyes widened in excitement, "That would be a dream come true!"

"Think about it and let me know" Minnie says, patting my shoulder, "It would be an honor to have you"

I watch her step away, glee filling my entire body. I turn to Asami and squeal, "This is incredible"

"Elena!"

I turn, Tadashi and Lillian walking up to us. Tadashi was grinning while his date carried a deep frown. I give him a small smile, "What did you think?"

"I think you are amazing!" He cheers, pulling me in for a hug, "It was incredible"

"Thank you" I say, "Did your father enjoy it?"

Tadashi frowns, "He wasn't able to come tonight, but he sends his best wishes. I will tell him about how wonderful you were"

My mind starts to turn. Aiko didn't come? Was the President even here? Aiko knew this would be a prime opportunity to strike.

"We should get you back to your dressing room" Asami says, breaking the beat of silence.

I nod, thinking hard. "Thank you for coming, Tadashi"

"We will see you later!" He calls, watching Asami lead me back to my dressing room. "Aiko isn't here?" I whisper, walking in stride with Asami.

"I know, it's odd" She mumbles, "Luckily I brought my speaker, I'll listen in through Spy Bug to see what is going on"

We turn the corner and I see Mako. A wide smile spreads across my lips as I rush into his outstretched arms. He brings me close to his chest, lifting me up gently.

"You did amazing" He says happily, "I was blown away"

I squeal, feeling him set my feet back on the ground. "I'm so happy you liked it, I was so nervous"

"You couldn't even tell," Mako says, his eyes bright.

"Would you two stop giggling?"

We turn, Korra waking up with her arms crossed as Iroh follows a few steps behind. Iroh pats my shoulder, complimenting my performance while Korra looks annoyingly at Mako.

"We have a job to do, remember?" She says with an irritated tone. "Where is Tadashi and the girl?"

"We saw them back stage" Asami says, "They invited us to an after party"

"Great" Korra says, clasping her hands together, "Finally, some action. Mako and I will go and scope it out."

"Tadashi is expecting me to be there" I say, "I think I can get him to open up"

Mako looks down at me, his arm wrapped protectively over my shoulders. "I don't think that is a good idea"

"Come with me" I smile gently, "Be my date, I feel safe with you by my side"

Korra groans, "I'm going to barf."

Mako rolls his eyes, then looks back at me, "Fine. But only for a little while"

Tadashi rented out a nightclub in the heart of the city. The room was crowded, full of people that didn't even attend the concert. I walk in with Mako, our hands interlocked. Iroh and Korra follow behind, both seemingly uncomfortable in such an atmosphere. Asami and Bolin went to her house to listen in on Spy Bug to see if they could track down Aiko.

I exhaled nervously, taking in the sight of the packed dance floor as the bass of the music made my head pound.

"Twenty minutes" I hear Mako yell in my ear over the music, "We are staying just twenty minutes"

"C'mon" I say, ignoring him. I yank his hand with mine, leading us through the thick crowd and up to the bar in the back of the room. We stand amongst people waiting for their drinks when Tadashi breaks through the crowd.

"El! You made it!" He smiles, wrapping an arm around me, "And you brought friends."

Tadashi holds in a grimace as he looks between Mako, Korra, and Iroh.

"We are a package deal" I say sweetly.

"Follow me, we have a VIP room in the back"

Tadashi leads us through the crowd and into a room behind a wooden door. There are black couches and a large table in the middle of the room, a waitress serving small cups of alcohol. Lillian sits on the couch in her gown beside three larger men.

Mako squeezes my hand, making me turn to glance at me. His eyes only said one thing: Trouble.

Chapter 24

Elena -

I had only been to a nightclub once. It was a few years ago in the Fire Nation. Vera and Iroh had hatched a scheme to throw a party at an up-and-coming spot in the capital and I was told to stand outside to look out for any Fire Nation guards.

Of course, a guard saw me and caught me before I was able to warn them, and we walked home with our heads hung in shame. Looking back it was worth the trouble. I remember feeling the bass of the music even from the sidewalk outside. I loved the way I felt it in my chest, it was exhilarating.

Now I was here legally, also with Iroh, but for a much different reason. I glanced over at him, curious if the same memory had crossed his mind.

I sit on the couch between him and Mako, a waitress pouring each of us a strong beverage. Tadashi sat across from us, Lillian lazily sipping her martini glass beside him.

"So, how did you hear about this place?" I ask, trying to defeat the sense of awkwardness in the air.

"A friend of mine owns it" Tadashi says, crossing his legs. "It just opened a few weeks ago"

"Will Aiko be joining us?" I ask curiously

Tadashi chuckles, "No, my father would never step foot into a place like this"

"That is too bad" I say, "I was hoping to see him"

"He has been busy with the investigation," Tadashi says, sipping his drink cooly. "They haven't found anything yet"

"Are they even looking?" Mako scoffs, a sour look on his face, "It has been weeks."

"It is a complicated case" Tadashi says, "Whoever is responsible did their due diligence. They really covered their tracks"

I glance over at Mako from the corner of my eye, seeing him squint at Tadashi thoughtfully. No one believed his story.

"I appreciate all he is doing" I lie, sipping my drink.

I swallow the liquid and feel it burn down my throat.

"I swear I know you from somewhere" Iroh says randomly, looking at Lillian thoughtfully. "Are you from the Fire Nation?"

Lillian looks at him unamused, her dark red lips still drawn in a frown, "I am. Born and raised."

Iroh pushed his eyebrows together in thought, trying to skim through his memories and place where he had seen this mysterious woman. Her ora reminded him of someone.. Was it a tutor he had? Perhaps a maid in the palace? Or maybe it was someone from his military career?

"So" I say, glancing at Tadashi, "When my family is found, what is next for you? Going back home?"

Tadashi thinks for a moment, "Yes, my father has set me up to assist him in his new business venture back in Ba Sing Se"

Business venture? Aiko is planning to start selling the formula?

"That sounds like fun" I say, "What is his business?"

"Pharmaceuticals" Tadashi says, "To be honest with you, I don't know much about it. He has kept the business a close secret."

"Why Ba Sing Se?" I ask, "Republic City is now the largest city in the world. Why would he want to leave?"

"I don't know," Tadashi says, sipping his cocktail. "Probably something to do with the laws. It is harder to start a business here with all the laws and regulations"

I swallow hard, catching Lillan's watchful gaze. I feel Mako's thigh touch mine, his glance settling on me.

"I'd love to learn more about his business" I say, voice even. "Perhaps you can arrange a dinner with the three of us?"

Tadashi smiles, "That is a genius idea, El"

- Mako-

The ride back to my apartment is silent. Elena riding in the passenger seat with her head turned to gaze out of the window. I take the time to reflect on our conversation with Tadashi. Ba Sing Se. That is where her father is planning to start selling her parents' formula. Shortly after Tadashi dumbly revealed his father's plan, Elena announced she had a headache and we left.

"We need to go to Ba Sing Se" Elena says, breaking the silence. "That is our first lead. We should take it"

"Ba Sing Se is dangerous" I say, "The city has been going downhill since Avatar Aang died, you shouldn't go."

"Mako" Elena says, turning to look at me sternly. "We have this discussion every time. I am going."

"Going to events with people to keep you safe and going to a crime riddled city like Ba Sing Se are very different situations, Elena" I say, "I don't think it is a good idea"

"Well, I don't care" She snaps, making me snap my head in her direction. She had never lost her temper with me before.

"What?" I say, looking at her quickly before bringing my attention back to driving. "What did you say?"

"I said, I don't care" She repeats, her voice growing more annoyed. "I appreciate you looking out for me, Mako, but it is getting exhausting. I am capable of taking care of myself"

"And how do you plan on doing that?" I snap back, "You can't even bend."

She closes her mouth tightly, her expression growing angrier. I frown, clearly I had gone too far.

"Elena" I sigh, "That isn't what I meant-"

"What? Just because someone can't bend doesn't mean they are defenseless, you know. People can take care of themselves without any stupid powers." She argues. "I am going to Ba Sing Se in the morning, with or without you."

I sigh again, gripping the steering wheel tightly.

"Fine" I say.

She knew just as well as I did that Ba Sing Se was nothing but trouble. But what could I do? I could never let her go alone.

- Unknown-

Nestled in the penthouse suite of the Grand Hotel in the heart of Republic City sat a woman at a vanity. The glow of the candle beside her flickered in the night as she examined herself closely in the mirror. She touched her skin softly, using the pads of her fingers to trace over her once wrinkled skin.

It was strange; going back to her youth. She remembered her life so vividly back then. How beautiful and powerful she was. Not only did she lose her golden chance to her moronic older brother, but she slowly lost her beauty as the years went by.

She lived in solitude all those years. Living on a small island off the coast of the Fire Nation. It was lonely, but that didn't bother her. It was the ever-aching reminder that she lost that drove her mad. She would look out the window and see fireworks in the sky in the distance, bitter as she watched the citizens celebrate another stupid holiday. It drove her crazy.

The war was hers to win.

As her body grew older, her anger grew stronger. Each passing day alone on the island made her feistier and hungrier for revenge.

She had just turned 89 when a visitor arrived on her doorstep. He was a clever man who had traveled far to make her a deal she could not refuse.

He would make her young again, all she had to do was capture the Shen family.

It took some convincing, as the woman was wise to any fool's tricks. But the man was able to produce undeniable proof. He had the secret to eternal life and endless youth.

Sure, she had to use a different name, Lillian. But she knew to bid her time. The best was yet to come.

So, there she sat. In the most expensive hotel in the lavish city her enemies built 70 years before. But this time, she wasn't going to let them win.

Princess Azula was twenty three again, back in her prime. And things were going to go her way.

A/N: I have been waiting for this chapter since I started writing this!!!! AZULA IS BACK. Things are about to get crazy.

Chapter 25

Mako -

I leaned against the counter, sipping a cup of warm tea. Elena was in the washroom, the hum of the shower coming through the walls. I sigh, looking into my cup of steaming liquid in thought. I knew I messed up in the car earlier, but she just didn't get it. I have been on crazy adventures the last few years, I know how dangerous this world can be. Elena had lived her life in the safety of palaces and hotels, she didn't understand how evil people can be.

I hear the shower squeak off, a beat of silence before the sound of the door sliding open. I quickly set the cup down, nerves pumping while I wait for her to open the door from the bedroom.

A moment later she appears, her night dress on as a towel is wrapped tightly around her hair. She doesn't smile, only leans against the door frame.

I sigh, feeling the awkwardness in the air.

"Elena"

"I need you to trust me, Mako" She says, speaking over me. Her voice was firm.

"And I need you to trust me" I argue back, "Elena, I know how scary this world can be. I have seen some really fucked up stuff and I don't want you to be around that"

"This entire situation is fucked up" She states, moving her hands as she speaks, "My father's best friend abducted my family. I can't be held back anymore, Mako. I have to be able to do something and you not argue with me everytime."

"I am not trying to argue with you" I defend, "Someone has to tell you the risks you are taking"

"I don't care!" she exclaims, tears pooling in her eyes. "I can't afford not to take risks, Mako. My entire world has been stolen from me. The people I had trusted most in my childhood have turned out to be my biggest enemies"

"I am just trying to look out for you" I say, my palms becoming hot. I could feel my anger slowly bubbling up.

"I don't need you to look out for me" She retorts.

I scoff, "Alright. Sure, Elena. And you'll get taken just like your family."

A wave of silence hits us both, regret instantly washing over my body, "Elena-" I start, but she is already turned away and in the bedroom. I watch the door slam shut, the sound echoing around me. I rub my hands over my face in frustration. She just didn't get it.

-Elena -

Mako didn't get it. It was infuriating. How could he not understand how much this meant to me? My entire family was in serious danger. We knew the police were not going to help. We were the only ones that stood between my family and death.

Why did he insist on standing in my way?

I look around the room quickly, my heart racing as anger pulses in my veins. He made me want to scream and cry all at once. I don't think I have ever been so angry in my life. I turn to the bag sitting on top of the cabinet and zip it open, pulling open a drawer and throwing some articles of clothing inside. I could not be around him tonight. I needed space. I needed freedom.

I don't take much time to think as I go to the washroom and throw some items inside before zipping it up and taking a deep breath. I open the door and see Mako on the couch, his head in his hands. I could feel the temperature in the room rising, his anger clearly affecting the space around us.

He looks up, his golden eyes lock to mine as I try to hold back tears of frustration.

"I am staying with Asami tonight" I state, not in the mood to offer more. He stands, a sigh escaping his lips.

"Elena, c'mon" He says, "You don't need to go all the way to Asami's"

"Yes, I do" I say, "Mako, I am done arguing with you. I am going"

"It's almost 3 in the morning" He states, sounding defeated, "Let's just go to sleep, Okay? I'll sleep on the couch. We can talk about this in the morning"

"There isn't anything to talk about" I say, crossing my arms over my chest. "I am going to Ba Sing Se."

He opens his mouth to say something but then stops, closing it again tightly. I give him a moment, expecting to hear him say something back but to my surprise he stays silent. He was right, it was late. We had both had long days. Clearly neither of us were at our best, but I couldn't stand the thought of not taking the chance to see if my family was in Ba Sing Se.

I move forward, slipping on my shoes and shrugging on my coat. I try my best to not look behind me as I unlock the door and step into the hallway. I close the door behind me and cover my mouth with my hand, trying to quiet the cry begging to escape. I had to get out of here.

Tears fog my vision as I walk down the stairs and out of the building, raising a hand to hail a cab. I half expected Mako to appear beside me, but he didn't. A cab pulls up, allowing me to slide into the backseat. I mumble off the address to Asami's and lean back into the leather seat and allow the tears to fall freely.

Almost an hour later we pull up the front gates of Asami's sprawling home on the outskirts of the city. I quietly toss a few coins to the driver and slide out, slinging my bag over my shoulder as I ring the bell on the gate.

A few minutes later a sleep-ridden voice sounds on the other side:

"Hello?"

"Asami" I say, "It's Elena"

"El?" She says, her voice sounding more awake, "What is it? Why are you here?"

"Mako and I had a fight" I say, "It's a long story"

The sound of the buzzer goes off and the gate opens, allowing me entry to her property. She greets me in the doorway, her hair striking up in random places as she squints at me through her sleepy haze.

"I'm sorry, El" she says, reaching to give me a hug. "Clearly it was a nasty fight if you came all this way"

"He has been suffocating me" I confess, "I just want to go to Ba Sing Se and see if we could find any clues."

"And Mako doesn't want you to go?"

"No" I say, sighing. I look around the entry of her house, trying to distract myself from the ache of anxiety.

"Well, let's get you settled. I think you'll feel better after some sleep" she says, guiding me up the curved stairs that lead to the upper level of her home. "I can draw you a bath if you want?"

"I think I'll just go to bed" I say, giving her a small smile. "Thank you for letting me stay here"

She gives me a small smile in return, opening the door to her guest bedroom, "It's what friends are for. Let me know if you need anything or want to talk."

"Thanks" I say, stepping inside and watching her shut the door, leaving me alone. I sit on the end of the bed, dropping my bag and begin to cry.

Nothing was going right.

The next morning Asami and I sit at the breakfast table, her chef serving us an array of delicious pastries. I still feel tired as I sip the mug of coffee, watching Asami flip through a notebook.

"I have a contact that I think will give us a ride to Ba Sing Se" she says, "Flying is much faster than taking a train"

I nod, trying to calm my still anxious mind. I had never fought with Mako and I hated the way it made me feel. I hardly got any sleep last night.

The phone rings on the hook, Asami standing and going to pick it up, the speaker held in her hand.

"Hi Mako" she says, giving me a look. I hear the muffled voice on the speaker, watching Asami's face react to his words. "Yes, she is here... No... Yes, I think she is.... Mako, I am not getting in the middle of this. You know she should go..... Well, I don't care...... That is up to Elena....Fine...Alright, I will have her call you... Bye"

She hangs up the phone and looks at me, "He wants you to call him, he says he is sorry and just wants to protect you"

"I know" I sigh, slumping in my chair, "It's just... too much sometimes"

"I know" Asami says, "Mako has always been this way. To tell you the truth, he has some serious abandonment issues, it comes from when his parents died. He just wants to make sure everyone he cares about is safe. He has a bad way of showing it, but he really loves you"

"Loves?" I say, "Mako loves me?"

Asami snorts, "Wait, did you not know?"

"Well...no" I say, cheeks flushing. "I mean, I know he likes me and all but..."

"Mako is so in love with you" Asami points out, "It's not an excuse for his actions but, it comes from a place of love.You guys should talk, I'd hate to see this get inbetween you to"

I nod, biting my lip between my teeth. Asami was right. We should talk. Now that we both had some time to cool off, we might be able to get it all worked out.

"Alright" I say, "I'll call him"

"Good" Asami smiles, "But not yet, we need to finish those chocolate pastries first"

www.ingramcontent.com/pod-product-compliance
Lightning Source LLC
Chambersburg PA
CBHW070356200726
48294CB00003B/936